STONEWALL INN
Michael Denneny, Ge

MW01182070

Buddies by Ethan Mo.

Joseph and the Old Man
by Christopher Davis

Blackbird by Larry Duplechan

Gay Priest by Malcolm Boyd

Privates by Gene Horowitz

Taking Care of Mrs. Carroll
by Paul Monette

Conversations with My Elders
by Boze Hadleigh

Epidemic of Courage by Lon Nungesser

One Last Waltz by Ethan Mordden

Gay Spirit by Mark Thompson, ed.

As If After Sex by Joseph Torchia

The Mayor of Castro Street
by Randy Shilts

Nocturnes for the King of Naples
by Edmund White

Alienated Affections
by Seymour Kleinberg

Sunday's Child by Edward Phillips

God of Ecstasy by Arthur Evans

Valley of the Shadow
by Christopher Davis

Love Alone by Paul Monette

The Boys and Their Baby by Larry Wolff

On Being Gay by Brian McNaught

Parisian Lives by Samuel M. Steward

Living the Spirit by Will Roscoe, ed.

Everybody Loves You by Ethan Mordden

Untold Decades by Robert Patrick

Gay & Lesbian Poetry in Our Time
by Carl Morse & Joan Larkin

by Larry Kramer

Personal Dispatches
by John Preston, ed.

Tangled Up in Blue
by Larry Duplechan

How to Go to the Movies
by Quentin Crisp

Just Say No by Larry Kramer

The Prospect of Detachment
by Lindsley Cameron

*The Body and Its Dangers and Other
Stories* by Allen Barnett

Dancing on Tisha B'av by Lev Raphael

Arena of Masculinity by Brian Pronger

Boys Like Us by Peter McGehee

Don't Be Afraid Anymore
by Reverend Troy D. Perry
with Thomas L.P. Swicegood

The Death of Donna-May Dean
by Joey Manley

Sudden Strangers
by Aaron Fricke and Walter Fricke

Profiles in Gay & Lesbian Courage
by Reverend Troy D. Perry
and Thomas L.P. Swicegood

Latin Moon in Manhattan
by Jaime Manrique

On Ships at Sea by Madelyn Arnold

The Dream Life by Bo Huston

Sweetheart by Peter McGehee

Show Me the Way to Go Home
by Simmons Jones

THE

Dream

Life

BO HUSTON

St. Martin's Press New York

Within this text, passages from *Death in Venice* by Thomas Mann are taken from the Borzoi Book edition, translated from the German by H. T. Lowe-Porter, published by Alfred A. Knopf, 1930.

Design by Judy Christensen

Library of Congress Cataloging-in-Publication Data

Huston, Bo.
    The dream life / Bo Huston.
        p.   cm.
    ISBN 0-312-08182-0 (hc)
    ISBN 0-312-09788-3 (pbk.)
    I. Title.
    PS3558.U7797D7   1992
    813'.54—dc20   92-24157
                                                                          CIP

First Edition: October 1992
First Paperback Edition: October 1993

10 9 8 7 6 5 4 3 2 1

The Dream Life

Holly

Prologue or epilogue. And keep the story simple.

I no longer feel dangerous. That was a thing of youth. Now I squint to see, the left eye hurts continually, and my throat rumbles (though I try to be discreet) with this cough, which is never complete, realized, gratifying. Something's gone terribly wrong, deep inside my spine, and knocked everything else off the tracks. Some of the fluids in me are soiled or crusted or something. It's a cruel, unfathomable sickness, originating in my childhood, which has just caught up with me. I am not loved by life.

It is usual for me to come here at this time, afternoon, and if it's cool I sit inside rather than at one of those outdoor tables. The coffee's excellent and strong. I have the newspaper and have smoked four or five cigarettes. My cane is leaning against my chair, close enough to be meaningful. The plants hang low here, and the café is too crowded with the small round marble-topped tables.

Beams and supports of dark, rough wood give the place a snug, cozy feel and it smells of bananas and liqueur. The music at this hour is not too loud or raucous (now it's Artie Shaw tunes). That stunning Ted or Tad or whatever his name is passed by me, carrying his dainty little custard pastry and his latte—"Well, *hello,* Holly," he said. I grunted, nodded. I can feel content just to watch: sexy men and boys in good moods and stylish, substantial women.

The kids these days have so many rings in their ears and noses. Heads are shaved, or partially shaved; sections of hair sliced and hacked and bleached white-yellow. Today's fashion has rhinestones and chains and thick black leather and exposed flesh.

I desperately miss Jed. My boy. Without Jed, there is no one who criticizes my criticism. No one to make assumptions about me.

A young man just asked me for a cigarette; I felt so awkward and nervous beside his sleekness. "Yes, yes, of course," I stammered and tapped one out of the pack. With a mild grin he thanked me, lit the cigarette, then turned his back to me to carry on with his friend. These boys are drinking good beer from bottles and gossiping. They wear bracelets. One has a bandana round his neck.

The young man is distraught. Or else he's faking it. "He called again this morning," he whispers.

The friend: "He did? No! And what did *you* say?"

I want to reach a conclusion in this vivid café. By the end of Artie Shaw's melancholy ballad and by the time I've finished my last crumpled cigarette and my coffee is cold, it is necessary that I achieve serenity. I must either be fully accepting of myself and the world or ready to turn my back on it.

This part of my life, and the future, I suppose I will label "After Jed."

Earlier, standing near the coffee bar, I overheard that messy Victoria telling Ingrid, emphatically: "Oh, no dear, I'm in AA now. I'm completely, absolutely on the wagon. Just a couple of martinis, very dry, late in the day."

And there's old Flanagan, pretending he does not recognize me. The professor, Flanagan. He glides through the doorway, erect, four fingers in his vest pocket with the thumb exposed, peering over the rims of his eyeglasses, edging past the tables to a booth at the back. Accompanying him is a young woman I've seen before, one of his students, I suppose. She has long, straight, black hair parted at the side; she's pale, wearing black and an overly large silver pin. At this graceful entrance one would almost expect applause or, better still, an obvious, awed hush in our little café. Flanagan and his student order iced teas and lean toward each other, knuckles to their mouths, conspiratorily.

I understand Flanagan's just had very good reviews of his newest novel. Flanagan's newest novel is called *Death in Venice.* Flanagan's protagonist is called Gustav Aschenbach—or von Aschenbach. Flanagan's Aschenbach becomes enchanted by a fair young boy who, as his golden-brown locks are swept across his smooth brow, gambols across the beach, poses under huge striped awnings framed by dark green water and banks of pearl-white sand; he wears sailor suits, sometimes wears nothing; he can be observed sitting obediently beside his tidy, impenetrable governess at tea. The boy is such a mystery, a construct that represents the "fatal gift." Aschenbach is majestically, beautifully transformed by desire, youth, love.

No, of course this is not Flanagan's book. I'm only

kidding. Flanagan is too stupid to write such a book. Flanagan's a steady, sincere cynic and it is not possible to be really cynical about love. Flanagan's a snooty, pedestrian, untalented little novelist. He does not seem to age, except that a concave red patch in his forehead becomes more distinct with the years. I could tell stories about Professor Flanagan. I've known him since I was eighteen or so. He hired me once to type some of his articles. I was lonely, I was frightened. I was not much of a typist, either. I was anxious to impress Flanagan, who, if he was not actually a famous writer, behaved like one, proudly displaying his handsome, limited-edition volumes of poetry. One was called *Blood and Fur*. He gave me a copy and signed it for me: "To Hollis Flood, a promising young man if ever there was one, L. Flanagan." (L. is for Leslie.) And he leered, winked, snorted as he showed me the inscription.

His set of rooms was comprised of absurd Victorian arrangements, cut-glass bowls turned at certain angles and lamps with figurines, the whole place draped with fussy, lacey things.

Flanagan watched me closely as he leant against his bookcase, fiddling nervously with his papers and sucking vodka. Then he'd say, every afternoon, "You going to be all right here working? I've got to take a nap. Come get me if you need anything," and he would retire to that convoluted, dangerous bed of his, piled with reference books; and he'd pass out.

I would finish my typing, organize the stacks of paper and carbons, straighten up the dining-room table, where I had done my work, and proceed quickly and quietly like a thoughtful bandit to Flanagan's bedroom door. Snuffling snores from the professor as he lay stretched out on his front. "I'm done," I'd say. "So, I'll be going."

Then Flanagan would sputter, rub his eyes, execute a lazy roll so that he was on his back and looking at me. His robe was open then. His penis was very large and purple and looked wet. The kick for Flanagan was the presumption of ordinariness in his exhibition—the whole bent of this harmless fantasy was that his nakedness was natural, easy, that his big, hard dick was just another thing about him. I knew intuitively not to react. "I guess I'm finished for today, Professor Flanagan."

"Ah, yes, thank you." He stretched. He rubbed his tan, bare chest and slid the hand down along his hip, down to his prick, which he took in his fist—natural, easy—and caressed. I stayed at the threshold between his dark living room (the wallpaper was maroon) and the airy bedroom (done in gray and tan). I watched him jerk and tug himself slowly and smoothly; then he'd beat harder, but not to real frenzy. It was an uncompelling performance and in only a moment he'd ejaculated on himself. Then he'd take the edge of the blanket and draw it over himself, curl into it on his side, nestle his head against a pillow. Then he'd put his thumb in his mouth and close his eyes. Like a baby boy.

I know that Flanagan's most vulnerable and thrilling instant was always that one—me standing in edgy muteness, the whole affected casualness, the context and mood of secrecy. And Flanagan, with his pathos and his thumb, was enacting shame.

What a simple thing it would have been for me to bark, "Really, what a sick old bird you are, you pervert jack-off queen. God!" Or I could take out a camera and click-click and laugh and run.

Oh, I could feel so dangerous then.

I despised Flanagan from the start. We did become lovers. He told me never to tell anyone, *anyone,* about his compulsion to suck his thumb, and I promised but told it all over town. Why do people set themselves up to be betrayed?

From Flanagan's masterpiece:

> It was an unfriendly scene. Little crisping shivers ran all across the wide stretch of shallow water between the shore and the first sand-bank. The whole beach, once so full of colour and life, looked now autumnal, out of season; it was nearly deserted and not even very clean. A camera on a tripod stood at the edge of the water, apparently abandoned; its black cloth snapped in the freshening wind. Tadzio was there. . . .

Right now, my legs sting too much for me to even begin to say how much I miss dear little Jed. And how much I am tormented with the lack of resolution: Who were we? Teacher and pupil, master and slave, or friends? Fagin and Oliver Twist. Lovers. We were certainly not like a father and son, in matching tan jackets, raking the leaves and tossing a ball and going for ice cream cones. Was that what Jed wanted? (In my deepest, most honest dreams, I was his mother.)

Where is he now? On some psychiatrist's couch, perhaps, cleaning up the mess I made. Giving his version of things—no doubt a much clearer, healthier version than mine.

I miss Jed with that saddest kind of grief: the way I miss my own childhood, my own self.

* * *

Asylum Street. Somewhere in New England; it was green and moist. Asylum Street met Factory Street, then curved, and at the end was a painted sign over an iron gate leading to a small courtyard of wooden benches and stunted, lazy trees. A yellow tomcat ducked and darted and hid. Shrill birds, especially in the morning, paraded fiercely across the smoky-gray, uneven bricks. My mama said the birds had disease. I was afraid of those birds.

I never can forget the two girls whose names were Olive and Ginger. They wore colorless, faded dresses and sandals, their hair was uncombed, their faces dirty. They whispered together, played on the ground with sticks and sometimes, pretending to be horses, they'd gallop and jump. I was obviously a subject for their secret discussions and titters.

One day I spied them sitting on a discarded wooden crate, swinging their legs. I went to them. "Do you live here?" I asked, twisting my fingers behind my back. Mama dressed me in short pants, hard-soled shoes with buckles, a white shirt and bow tie, and my blond hair was cut short and patted flat.

They looked at each other, open-mouthed, burst into laughter. "Hey, kid," Olive (the tough one) demanded, "do *you* live here?"

"We live with my aunt. Over there"—I pointed— "at the end of the road. But, my mama works here."

Again, they laughed and Ginger wondered what my mother did here. I said she was a nurse and came to take care of the sick people. Does your mama wear a uniform? She did. Does she give shots when people go mad? I did not know.

One of those shrill birds, possessive and peevish, soared past my head and I cried out in fear, drawing my fists to my chest, which made the girls howl with laughter. Ginger said, ''Don't you like the peacock?''

I *knew* it was not a peacock, but I kept silent and still.

Inside, the corridor was wide, dimly lit by brass lamps along the walls. The floor was pale yellow cracked stone. I sat on a wooden bench, waiting for Mama. I could see her vaguely through the glass panel on her office door. I always tried to stay awake, but the coolness, the echo softened me. Mama would come, finally, and shake my knee. ''Time to go, sweetie,'' she'd say and lead me through the hazy, deep halls, out the side entrance doors, which she would lock with a set of three keys.

Mama would undo her hair and smoke a cigarette as she held my fingers tight in her hand. At night, with fast winds bending and shaking the giant trees, we made our journey to the end of Asylum Street, to a narrow, unmarked lane; there our three-room house stood, crookedly, glowing gloomily in the yellow porch light. The roads here were unpaved, strewn with pebbles and dust and twigs.

Just crossing Factory Street, heading toward our house, I remember there was a billboard sign, old and faded, illuminated by white bulbs: a smiling Indian in feathers said DRINK ORANGE CRUSH.

Aunt Joy liked to play the radio, but it gave Mama a headache. Aunt Joy made us supper when we got home: tuna-fish casserole or creamy vegetable soup from a can or macaroni and cheese from a box. Mama, still in her white uniform, chewed and sighed in a quiet, sad, tired rhythm, the way she did all things.

Aunt Joy would tell us about a man she'd met that day on the street or in the Woolworth's, who was fresh to her. She'd talk about the sales on shoes or hats. Aunt Joy collected catalogs from all the colleges and went through them, circling the courses she'd like to take. "Here's one all about the history of Venice. Venice is such a beautiful place. I'd love to go there someday. And if I ever do go there someday, what I really should do is enroll in this course and learn all about the history of it."

From my earliest days, I could sense what Mama thought of her sister Joy. That Joy was a stupid dreamer, useless, too sexy, too pretty. "Some people are just loved by life," Mama would say dismally of Aunt Joy.

Aunt Joy put me to bed at night, told me not to be scared of the dark.

"Is there something under the bed?" I'd ask her.

"Now, what would be under your bed, little one?"

"Maybe a lunatic escaped from the asylum and came to hide under there."

As she settled the blankets over me, ash from the cigarette between her lips crashed silently on her knee, and she brushed it away. "Now, Holly. No lunatics have escaped. And if any of them did, why would they come all the way over here?"

I would be calmed by Aunt Joy's assured logic and her soft hands folding the blanket under my chin. Later, from the front room, I could hear a gentle slap-slap of cards on the coffee table as Mama and Aunt Joy played gin. Aunt Joy would turn on the radio, but it gave Mama a headache. I would trace the faded diamonds on the wallpaper with my finger.

I wished to tell Mama that I did not want to go with her tomorrow. Those birds frightened me. Those girls, Olive and Ginger, frightened me.

(Everything frightens me.)

The house would soon go dark. Mama would close the

door to her room. Aunt Joy might grab her bags, get a taxi, fly off without a word to some magnificent college in Venice. And out of my closet would lurch the gigantic, menacing, feathered Indian lunatic, smiling, drinking orange sugary soda, ready to kill me. I am not loved by life.

Jed

Holly says you always lose the one thing you really love. Could be a person, could be talent or beauty, or some possession or pet, or maybe it will be home. That's inevitability, Holly says. And the world is in this mad dash toward its own destruction: technology and modern art and lack of morality and everything are spreading some kind of vicious disease. No one has good manners anymore. That's how Holly talks. He talks like he's making a speech or something.

Holly doesn't frown or smirk or look mean. Holly just has his philosophy—"benevolent doom," he calls it—and I think he really does like to startle people, to shock.

He's an individual. I know that much. He's a real character. On my fifteenth birthday last June, Holly was speaking rather frankly about teenage suicide. "Do you know the suicide rates for kids have jumped two hundred percent in the last decade?" he asked. "You need to take a good look at that, Jed. They were saying"—Holly is always listening to the radio talk shows—"they were telling the warning signs: changes in mood, changes in behavior, grades going down, a kind of withdrawal these kids go through." Holly said he would never *encourage* me to take my own life, but such an action would be understandable. See, he likes to shock. He said he often wishes he'd killed himself when he was a lad.

Holly uses words like *lad*. He's rather old-fashioned in his own way. He calls the stereo a hi-fi, and he's always playing weird jazzy organ music or sad opera on it. To Holly, Kennedy Airport is Idlewild and PBS is educational TV. I guess I'm old-fashioned too, actually, but in a different way, and maybe Holly recognized some piece of himself in me.

See, I didn't get on too well in school. Mostly the problem was I didn't have any friends. Ever since around fourth grade—Holly says I was probably raped or something when I was in fourth grade and that I've blocked it out, but that it's the root of all my problems—ever since then I would fake being sick so I could stay home from school. My mother—I call her by her first name, Lila, I always have—anyway, she caught on to the whole thing. One morning, she called me into the dining room; she was sitting at one end of this enormous shiny table we had, and I was at the other, this tiny boy in a bathrobe.

"Now. *What* is it that doesn't feel well?" she asked.

"Sore throat," I answered. I always claimed I had a sore throat.

"I see. A sore throat. It seems you very frequently have a sore throat."

I just nodded or something. I could tell she was on to me. By ten years old you already know all about lying and manipulation, etc. Isn't that sad?

Lila lit a cigarette, but there was no ashtray so she dropped the dead match onto the table. She crossed her legs. I guess she was going out somewhere because she was dressed in this smart little black suit and high-heeled shoes. She was always going to some committee meeting or brunch or whatever. That's kind of how Lila spent all her time, doing charity-type pursuits. Her pocketbook was on the floor next to her, leaning against her chair. "I want you to tell me what's going on," she said sternly. Just then her third husband, Mr. Sylvestre, the bald one, walked through the dining room, straight through, on into the kitchen, and didn't even look at my mother or me. I remember thinking how strange that was. Mr. Sylvestre was without a doubt the strangest of her husbands.

My mother said, "I *know* you aren't really sick, Jed. So what is all this not-going-to-school business?"

Here was one of those weirdly important moments, when everything goes foggy, your ears pop, when you have to make a fast decision by pure instinct or something. So I knew I could just go on and on with my fake coughing and say how I didn't feel well; or I could try the truth. My mother was tapping her index finger on the table, drawing on her cigarette and blinking at me, waiting for me to answer. I guess she was trying to be soft or gentle or whatever. She was trying to urge me along with her help-ful-concerned look, which I'd seen on her face before; but she only appeared furious like always.

My lower lip started to quiver, the way little kids' lips quiver when they're about to cry. "Nobody likes me at school," I stammered. "Everyone is mean to me." So there, I'd said it, right?

My mother had her tense-squinting look then, and I thought she must not have understood what I meant. So then I really sobbed. "I don't have any friends," and I lowered my head. Tears fell onto my robe, which, I remember, had cute little monkeys on it, and I watched the dark patches of wetness spread. Lila didn't say anything for quite a while; I just looked across at her.

Her lips were tight, she was gazing at this framed thing by Paul Klee or somebody, which hung over her antique oak hutch. Had she even heard me? Then she looked directly at me and said, "Well. Neither do *I*."

I had blue blue eyes when I was a little kid; and then they turned sort of greenish-gray. I was trying to tell Lila, my mother, the truth—that I was lonely, that I felt scared, how sad and lonely and scared I was because I didn't have any friends, and she only could say, "Well, neither do *I*." So, I've always wondered if that was true, if she really had no friends either and felt so alone. It would explain a lot about Lila, actually. Or maybe she just said that without thinking, just said it. I figured out that day how you can't trust people, and my eyes went from pretty-little-boy-blue blue to this kind of greenish-gray color they are today.

Our flight to Los Angeles was dreamy and smooth. It was my first time on an airplane, if you can believe that. Lila was always flying off somewhere—New York, San Francisco, Chicago, etc.—but she never took me, not even once. I didn't so much want to go where she was going, and I didn't really want to be with her or anything; but I did want to ride in a plane. I remember standing at the window, holding the hand of some maid or chauffeur or whatever, watching the plane make a slow turn with lights blinking on the wings, watching these handsome, tough guys loading everybody's bags.

Anyway, Holly complained about the stewardesses—their hair, their high-pitched voices, their phoniness and condescension. One of them asked Holly to put his cane in the overhead luggage compartment and he refused, and they argued some, and then the head stewardess or whatever you call them came over. I just looked out the window. Holly can be so embarrassing in public. He is actually rude to anyone in a servile position: waiters, drivers, sales clerks.

Holly doesn't even really need the cane. He told me the truth about it last year, late one night, during a thunderstorm.

"It's a ruse," Holly explained. "It's like a disguise. Oh, the legs do hurt once in a while, but it isn't unbearable and I have my little pills for that. What fascinates me is how differently one is treated when one is thought to be an invalid. I can demand special attention with this thing." He lifted up his cane like a prize; it's a shiny wooden stick with a slick, silver, rounded handle. "I love the sympathetic gazes. I love how people look at the cane, then at my legs, to discover the infirmity, then to my face to see if I have caught them looking. Which I always have. I always look right back at them."

I told Holly I bet there were hundreds, thousands of people who actually need canes to walk and that they would trade anything just to throw theirs down the way Holly could.

"Well . . ." Holly blinked his eyes lazily. "Let them."

That's what he's like sometimes, that's his way. He lacks compassion. He's sort of a hard person to like. Maybe I'm the only one in the world who really does like Holly.

I was thirteen when we met and it seemed he towered

above me. I thought he might be eight feet tall or something, but he's just under six feet. He has short, bristly,
reddish hair. He is rather thin, with square shoulders, and
his legs seem too long for his body. I actually forget
sometimes how weird he looks, I'm used to Holly now;
and then we'll be walking somewhere and I'll see a little
kid, holding its mother's hand or something, sucking
its thumb or whatever, and just staring at Holly, staring,
and the kid's mother will say, "Don't stare." Which always gives me a shudder feeling—like I hate everyone for
one horrible second; I hate the mother, the kid, Holly,
and me.

But Holly's face is beautiful. Beautiful like an old-time
woman movie star almost. He has those huge brown eyes,
set wide, and pale, pale skin, a curvy chin and pointy
cheekbones, as though his face were one of those fine,
powdery-white marble sculptures.

The thing about Holly—the thing about me and Holly,
I should say—is that we've always understood each other.
He seems mean, hard, bitter, and it's embarrassing a lot of
the time, it's hurtful sometimes. But it's so much an act,
and you can't know that unless you've been with him the
way I have. He's really joking half the time. Playing a part
he wrote for himself in a play that he's directing. And
something makes me think this has been going on since he
was a little kid. There's a lot of pain inside Holly, I know
that. Holly is thirty-three years old now. He's suffered so
much—he was raised by this aunt he really loved, but his
mother was depressed, and he's told me all about when
he was little and he had to hang around this weird insane asylum where his mother was a nurse and everything.
And his mother had some kind of terrible breakdown

herself and everything, and finally she just kind of shut herself up in her bedroom and hardly ever came out. Her hair
got long and gray. But he did love the aunt. It sounds like
his childhood was rather dark and lonely. Then when he
was my age, he ran away, and all through his teens he
was on the streets, hustling, drinking, etc. He used to be a
pretty heavy-duty drug addict, actually; he's told me about
taking a lot of speed and his heroin habit and then being
on a methadone program, and all this was a long time
ago and everything, I know. I'm just saying, Holly's had a
hard life.

See, Holly *has* to wear a mask. And so he lacks compassion. I once even said, "Holly, the thing about you, you
lack compassion."

He said, "That's fine, dear, that's terribly perceptive
of you. Why don't you have compassion for both of us?"

Now I was by the window, Holly was in the middle
seat, and an elderly black woman all in red was sitting on
the aisle. She told us her name: Mrs. Mann. She had a huge
red hat perched on her lap and a red bag at her feet. She
had asked for cognac and they told her it was not served,
and she and Holly discussed all the shortcomings of the
airline and compared these stupid stewardesses with all the
other stupid stewardesses they'd come across, and also
waitresses and nurses and clerks. Holly was being too loud,
but he really had Mrs. Mann howling with laughter.

The sun was going down, casting thick, golden beams
against the silver wing, and the sky became dark blue, then
black. I fell asleep. My head was against the thick plastic
window and the vibrations and constant hum sounded deep
inside my ears.

In the dream, Holly was there. Walking a few steps

ahead of me, with his small limp. Then there was steam. Then a glass bottle rolled down some steps and broke, but there was no sound. More steam, in bursts, and someone was crying. I woke up.

"I heard that," said Holly in a nasty tone.

"What?" I was rubbing my eyes with my fingertips. "Did I say something?"

"Yes, goddamn it. You said 'My mother.' " Holly looked at me in this rather disapproving way, very stern, his right eyebrow curved up in an arch.

"It was . . . oh, I had a dream. Steam from a train, something breaking."

Mrs. Mann fussily undid her seat belt, got up, walked down the aisle toward the lavatory.

"You had your chance," Holly said, and he looked straight ahead, folded his arms over his chest. "You've had plenty of chances now. You've always been a free agent as far as I'm concerned. I certainly never wanted to keep you if it was against your better judgment."

That's Holly's way. Everything's a challenge, a contest; he'll pout and sulk; it's his will against my will, only usually I don't even know what is at stake. I guess maybe I *never* know what is at stake for Holly.

"It was only a dream, Holly. I can't help what I dream. Just because I have a dream——"

"God knows it's *your* life——"

"Just because I dream something doesn't mean I don't want to stay with you."

"Hand me my pills, will you? They're in the bag under your seat."

See, that's just Holly, that's just his way. He's really a character.

Holly

I left Flanagan on a wet afternoon. He had just received advance copies of his preposterous book of essays, *Fleece Them!* And as I headed out with my suitcase in my hand and several of Flanagan's credit cards in my wallet, he called after me, "Wait! It's dedicated to you!"

So, when I was eighteen or so, I lived for some months in glamorous Beverly Hills. Dick the famous actor took me in, gave me my own room—a corner room with gorgeous leaded windows that overlooked the garden—and the place had antique mahogany furniture, rose-colored wallpaper, squat brass table lamps with cloth shades. He allowed me to use one of the cars. He bought me clothes: wool sweaters in pastel colors, tailored slacks, crisp shirts, and ties and gloves and overcoats. Dick the famous actor's real passion was shoes, though, and after some weeks I had a closet quite full of them. And then I, too, developed this love of shoes; I absorbed his delight, his fascination with them, and understood its logic: each pair demanded a different stride, a different stance. Shoes are the foundation and they define the entire attitude, the worldview. With endless choices regarding shoes, one can adopt a new, complete personality. What shall I be today? Elegant, energetic, thoughtful, needy or assured or flighty? It all depends on shoes. (At twenty, of course, my limp was not yet so pronounced. Today I can only wear plain, black, Navy oxfords.)

Dick the famous actor liked to dress me up and parade me around, but he mostly liked for me to stay at the pool, bare and greasy from suntan lotion, stretched out lazily on one of the wooden deck chairs. He brought me cocktails. He brought me magazines. He liked to serve me. Serving me was Dick the famous actor's way of being served *by* me.

And then I was kept by another actor; and then I was in a few porno films; and then I had an affair with a doctor; and then I lived for a while in Berlin, then in Paris; and then I went back to Dick the famous actor, and by this time we each had a considerable heroin habit. I stole the most expensive of his shoes. I stole his car. I left town. Someone fell in love with me. Someone else fell in love with me. Is anyone listening?

(And then one night I saw a reflection of myself. It was my twenty-first birthday. I was staying with a Dutch guy in Manhattan, and as I was closing the medicine cabinet after searching it for drugs to steal, there were my eyes in the mirror. So tired and sad, like chocolate melting on the sidewalk of Asylum Street, like Mama's hurt, resigned eyes. This vision of myself came upon me quite unexpectedly, caught me in the act—myself as thief, hustler, liar, and, somehow most bruising, myself as tireless, rushed, infinitely hungry. Except for red hair and white skin, I could see no reminder of Aunt Joy, my heroine, in my reflected image. Nothing of her in me. Once there was something of hers I wanted. Once I had sat cross-legged on the floor, she had sung to me, I had loved her. "What is the *matter* with you?" I asked the thin, dead face in the mirror. I almost cried but was in too much of a hurry to cry.)

It is terrifying, I guess, to be without any values. Moral direction, however it is measured, described, interpreted, makes us feel safe. So, for that to be absent is fundamentally painful. So, that I am a man who says, "No—I do *not* know—I do not *even* care—"makes me some kind of monster. A modern monster.

We are nowhere near Armageddon, despite the asinine ramblings of the bible doomsayers. We're not even close to real decay. We'll know it's all over when people simply do not believe in *anything* anymore.

In a highway restaurant outside of Toledo, Ohio—those old days seem so long ago, and I remember them sadly, fondly—a black-and-white television, perched precariously above the counter, blared a news report of an epidemic: little old ladies were being brutally assaulted and robbed on Toledo's streets. The newscaster—some fag with a concerned pancake-face and stiff hair—gave a sketchy description of a pair of thugs and warned elderly women citizens not to go out alone or at night.

Jed had stopped eating his cheeseburger to listen to the report. "God, that's awful. Isn't that awful, Holly?"

"I don't know."

"No, really. Beating up little old ladies?"

"It happens, Jed. All kinds of things happen."

"But . . . I know that, but, I mean, some of them are bad. That's all I'm saying."

I told him to finish lunch. Later, in the car, this dialogue—which thrilled me, really, but which I pretended was only an irritation—continued.

"Holly, can't you admit that there are wrong, bad, immoral types of things that happen?"

"No. I won't admit that at all. There are just things that happen."

"What about child abusers and alcoholics and racists, et cetera?"

"Don't use the word *et cetera*. All right, yes, there are such people. Are you looking for someone to blame for something?"

"No, I'm just trying to say . . . well, what about like creepy things like incest or whatever?"

"Yes. That exists."

"What about if they take some man and put electrical wires on his dick and shock him and then nail his balls to a wall?"

"Well, Jed, what *about* that?" By now I was somewhat exasperated.

He raised his hands and slapped his thighs in desperate frustration—almost like he was trying to teach a stupid little boy the alphabet. "I mean, come on, wouldn't you say that would be a really creepy, gross, awful thing?"

"Maybe. Maybe some men would actually like it."

"Now you're just playing games or something, Holly, you're just trying to seem like you don't care about anything." Which I thought was quite perceptive. His beauty was absolute at that moment—the pouting lips, the black hair fallen across his brow, the eyes: green for a second, gray for a second. By Toledo, I loved Jed.

* * *

Oh, no. Here is Julius.

"Holly? Oh my *God,* it *is* you. May I join you, dear?" I nod at the chair across from me and Julius settles himself into it. One has to be in just the right mood for Julius, something specific, predisposed to quick bantering and superficial observations. Julius has his own unique world-view—but then, at the same time, I think it is a very obvious, predictable one. He is despicable, he is conservative, bigoted, petty, somehow not even real; and yet, because he makes no apologies, he can be incomparably entertaining. The breadth of his ability and willingness to insult is often delightful. When I am at all fragile, though, I simply cannot handle Julius.

"Oh, I see Miss Flanagan is here with her bevy of academic types. Don't you just hate that? So, how *are* you, anyway?" Julius has a canary-yellow, floral-print ascot and his hair is streaked with fake blond color. "I haven't seen you in ages, darling. I was thinking about you just the other day because those two lesbian sisters who always give the art parties had a little dinner, and I looked around, looked around, I was asking people, 'Where's Holly?'

"I'll tell you the truth," Julius confides, "I wondered if you hadn't gotten AIDS and dropped dead. *So* glad to see you're not dead, dear."

I smile. "No. Somehow I managed to avoid that particular virus."

"It's a crapshoot, sweetheart."

"It is. It surely is."

"Anyway," he continues. "You know that new boy-friend Wayne has been dragging around everywhere? Well, my dear, turns out he's a heroin addict. They haven't had sex in months. *Months.* Wayne's one of those obsessive types, he likes to take care of the poor, beautiful losers. There was that other one named Lawrence or something who sold all of Wayne's books, you remember him. All Wayne's priceless signed first editions, worth a fortune—I mean Burroughs, Isherwood, and all those faggot poets and everyone—just *sold* them. Wayne's a mess. I told him so. I said, 'Wayne, darling, you're tiring out all your friends. Everyone thinks you're a stupid cunt.' "

Julius has eyes that are never fully open, the lids linger, droop. He says I'm looking so well these days—which is certainly not true—and I return the compliment with a strained smile. All of my smiles are strained.

He sips an ominous-looking drink, a cloudy copper-colored concoction. He lights a cigarette. "I guess by now you've heard what happened to Conway."

"I heard he had died. In Paris, was it?"

"It was Berlin, my dear. *Not* a pleasant place to die. You know, Conway was a diabetic but also a vicious alcoholic. So, yes, of course, he died, yes, but have you heard the whole *story*?"

I do not reply.

Julius leans in closer, affecting a strategy of cozy confidence. "It was a suicide. *Sort* of. Conway was involved in some very shady things, namely selling syringes to horrid black-market people. Selling drugs, too, and he kept riding back and forth to Europe on the Concorde, and he hooked up with this very, very wealthy Brazilian woman called Belva or something and her Jewish husband and they were just about as reckless as you can be with all the drugs and the money and everything. This was last year. I was living with Peter—who by now, you know, was never faithful to me for one day, not for one goddamn day. And he *claimed* to be an artist and he kept talking about his art dealers and

his galleries. He was doing these huge canvases with pictures of erect penises in *hideous* colors, just awful, no
integrity or depth.

"But the story of poor Conway. This Belva and her
rich Brazilian Jewish husband hired Conway—if you can
call it hiring. They convinced him to write a play for them.
It was supposed to be a pornographic musical, a sado-
masochistic thing, with lesbians and masturbation. You
know. And all those kinds of things are *so* tired, but
Conway was in such a state he'd do any goddamn thing for
money. So, this Belva and her husband commissioned Conway to work on this play and they made big promises—it
would be done for German television, a lot of money was
supposed to be involved. And Conway, naturally, was all
excited, just thrilled, and gloating and bragging. He'd say,
'Oh, I have to work on my "piece." ' He kept calling it
his 'piece.' Isn't that vulgar?

"Well, my dear— Oh, sweetheart"—he curls a finger to flag a waiter—"let me have another of these, will
you? Anyway, these crazy Brazilian Jewish monsters ended
up locking Conway in a tower of a castle—and I am *not*
kidding, a real tower in one of those insane castles in the
middle of the German countryside, in the goddamn middle
of nowhere. And they *wouldn't* let him out. It was like a
sick sort of game. They didn't give him an ounce of food.
Just orange juice and amphetamine, amphetamine and orange juice. And they forced him to write and write, this
pornographic musical play. Conway worked away, worked
away, and then Belva and her husband would say, 'Oh, this
isn't right, Conway, this isn't what we had in mind,' and
he'd write and write some more. Three weeks of this,
mind you.

"It was all a big joke to Belva and her Brazilian Jew,

you know. They love to torment people. They love to come up with these ideas and manipulate everyone into working on their atrocious projects. Not that Conway didn't have his part in this whole arrangement. He wrote me one letter. From the tower of this castle. I don't know where I've put that letter, but it was *fascinating,* just utterly *fascinating.* He told me how he was so loaded on the speed they kept giving him and they wouldn't let him leave, and then he said, well, he wasn't sure he really even wanted to leave. Things like that. He wrote that they wouldn't allow him clothing and it was very cold, but being naked and so cold was helping him to write this play. And this Belva person would come in his little tower room, the little garret or whatever it was, to tell him that she did not like what he'd written so far, it wasn't right. And then this brute woman would say, 'Don't you want to get it *right,* Conway?'

"Anyway, the end result of this sick, sick, *sick* story is that Conway slaved away, a virtual prisoner, and eventually one day he simply hopped out the tower window. Or, rather, there's some question about whether he jumped himself or was pushed by Belva or the Brazilian Jew or both. He was naked when he was found all twisted up on a pile of rocks at the bottom of this castle. So, naturally, there are any number of revolting scenarios that run through one's mind. But Belva told everyone, from the coroner's office to the cocktail parties, that Conway was just terribly depressed and vitamin-deficient and had just impulsively killed himself in this fit of despair. No one knew what to believe, so the whole thing got very neatly wrapped up.

"Well, as you know, Holly, Conway was absolutely my oldest and dearest friend, so this whole episode was enormously traumatic for me. And now some German queen wants to write a book about the whole thing, like a fictionalized account of this business, and Belva was talking to André and some other people about how she's considering the movie options. *Movie options.* Can you imagine? Have you ever heard anything so grotesque?''

I'm thinking, Oh, well, yes, yes I have.

Jed

Holly was lots of things to me in my life, but first and most he was my teacher. We went through all this stuff, the traveling and fighting, all the love we had and stuff, but some little piece of me always still did think of him as my teacher, always will.

See, what happened, by the time I reached the eighth grade, Lila had had it. That's what she said. "I have just *had* it with you." The remark didn't sting much by that time. By thirteen years old I was pretty tough, actually.

I'd stopped faking sickness; now I just wasn't bothering to show up to classes. I was hanging out with this weird, ugly girl named Ceil who had thick glasses and buck teeth. Her ambition was to be a prostitute. Also, she was pretty seriously into witchcraft—she read a lot about it and said these little incantations and everything. Once she put a hex on her stepfather. Ceil and I would smoke cigarettes

together under the bleachers and drink wine. Ceil threw
up a lot.

Actually, it was a rather upper-class sort of world I was
raised in. Everyone lived in these ranch-type houses, but
not the tacky kind. The sprawling, rich-looking kind with
wide, winding driveways. I thought those driveways had a
rather mournful sense about them, actually. All the kids'
parents were divorced, all the kids got stoned on something or other. The kids were fucking all over the place or
whatever and one time, even, a teacher at the high school
got fired for fucking a girl student. It was a decadent
community, I guess you'd say. Way ahead of its time.

Ceil and I pored over dirty magazines—not like those
glossy kind you get in drug stores, but the really sleazy
ones with she-males and ads for dildos and everything, and
we'd just be stoned and laughing. One day—we were
pretty stoned, because we'd taken ten or fifteen of those
over-the-counter caffeine pills—I dared Ceil to take her
shirt off in the cafeteria and she did. She had these white
white breasts with pink ends, and she just sat there, half-
naked. The other kids were pretty damn shocked and
startled, I must say. I must say, I was a pretty manipulative
sort of kid, I think, daring Ceil to do something like that.

Also, I was pretty much what you might call chronic
as far as masturbation goes. What I was doing was masturbating in different locations; for some reason I was really
fascinated with the idea of masturbating in all the rooms of
the house, the backyard, the garage, the bathroom at
school. When we went out anywhere—Lila took me to
plays sometimes, and sometimes to restaurants, once in a
while even to a dinner party of one of her friends—I'd
find the bathroom and masturbate. Partly, I was fascinated
with my own dick, which is kind of a weirdly embarrassing

thing to admit. Every time I saw it or touched it—every time—I'd get that jabbing jolt of pleasure. Which I can't really explain. And so then masturbating in these different places made the whole sensation stronger, more intense, dreamier, etc. I thought maybe I was a pervert, but then that idea kind of got me excited, too.

I don't know. I think masturbating all over the place was, actually, in a weird way, comforting. To be in a new place, doing an old thing. Masturbating was comforting because it was familiar, like the only really familiar thing in my whole life. Later, when I told Holly about my perversion, he said it was like a dog marking.

So, my mother—"I have *had* it with you." Not because of masturbation; she didn't know about all that. It was too many notes home from teachers, too many phone calls from the principal and vice-principal and all those types of people, and finally they expelled me from the school, which was a snooty private middle school so they could kick you out if they wanted to.

Lila was sitting on her brand new mauve sofa, which cost five million dollars or something, swirling her martini around and sucking her cigarette and saying how disappointed in me she was. See, the principal had called her that afternoon, right in the middle of one of her board of directors things, for the art museum or whatever. "I *don't* suppose it even *occurred* to you that I was in a *very important* meeting. I don't *suppose* it matters to you at *all.*" And she went on and on about how inconsiderate I was, always had been, etc., and finally I couldn't take it, a sense of the injustice of it all overwhelmed me. I really think kids are much more sensitive to unfairness.

I said, rather loud, "Look, do you think I like to be messing up in school? Hasn't it ever occurred to *you* that maybe I'm *troubled* or something?'' See, it was just like back in fourth grade, way back, seemed like centuries before, when I tried to ask my mother for help, to tell her the truth about me.

"Oh, you're troubled are you?" Her legs were tucked under her bottom on the mauve sofa and she began rubbing the soles of her stockinged feet with her hand. "Troubled? Troubled? Well, we've all got troubles, mister. I mean, if you think you've got troubles now. . . ." She was having a fit or something, she was all red. She stubbed out her cigarette, her hand was trembling, and then she closed her eyes and took a few huge breaths. She whispered to herself, with her eyes closed, "I am serene. I am serene. I am serene." See, Lila had joined this weird group where they meditated and told themselves they were serene all the time, even though they were all practically certifiable neurotics or whatever.

"All right," she finally said to me, when she'd opened her eyes. "Here's what you're going to do. You're going to go up to your room and clean it."

I must have rolled my eyes or something. I mean, her solution to everything was always to clean.

"That's right, mister. And I don't mean straighten up or tidy up. You *clean*, mister. Spotless. That bed made. Every item of clothing folded or hung. The rugs shaken. The windows washed. All of it *clean*. Like your life depends on it, mister. Understand?" She lit another cigarette and then she took this box that was on the floor beside her, opened it fiercely, and inside was a ridiculous black hat with a wide brim and a white sash, and she put on the hat. She just put on the hat. I thought maybe she'd gone crazy, right in front of my eyes. Her kid's got all these problems, drinking and smoking and hanging around with crazy Ceil, and then he gets expelled; and all Lila could think to do was have me clean my room while she sat alone wearing a new hat. "I am serene," she fumed.

So, there were quite a few more messy scenes involving my mother, myself, and her fourth husband, Mr. Levine. Mr. Levine used to be a rabbi but then he invented a little gadget that increases the efficiency of Xerox machines or something. He became a millionaire. They'd have these private talks in their bedroom about what should be done with me, and then they'd call me in. Mr. Levine would stand next to the bureau, fiddling with his cuff links and whatever. He must have felt rather weird, actually. I mean, he hardly knew me, and here he was all embroiled in this adolescent stuff. Anyway, Lila did all the talking. I just sat picking at threads on her expensive chaise lounge.

Finally, Lila hit on a solution. "What we've decided, Jed, is to arrange a tutor for you. This person will come right here to the house and you will study privately. It seems you are too distracted at school"—she took a violent drag of her cigarette—"you're restless. Obviously, you're more advanced than the other students, and the teachers do not challenge you. So, Morris"—that was Mr. Levine—"and I have agreed that a tutoring situation would be appropriate for right now, for this stage of your education. We have talked it over at some length and . . . Will you *stop* picking at that upholstery!" she barked at me, and I jumped, and Mr. Levine jumped too.

Anyway, so this is how Hollis Flood and I came to meet. That day seems like so long ago. I was standing in the kitchen with our new maid, Eliza. She was practically only a kid herself, seventeen or so. She'd just been working for us a couple of weeks. Eliza was Amish. Lila hated her and made sarcastic remarks, paid her next to nothing. Eliza was nice enough but real timid. She wore a plain gray dress and a white apron and white bonnet. I don't really know what the Amish life is like or anything. I mean, I know they make cheese and everything. Eliza walked in on me naked in the bathroom once, and I even had half a hard-on, and she screamed, she literally screamed, she literally went running down the hallway, threw the towels she'd been carrying, and kind of pulled her apron up over her head.

Anyway, that morning, I had my ear against the kitchen door, trying to hear Lila interviewing this new tutor. They were in the living room. She'd say something too soft, he'd say something, and then she would laugh. And she kept saying, "How delightful, Mr. Flood." "That's most impressive, Mr. Flood."

I never have found out exactly what tricks he used on my mother—or, actually, what tricks she used on him. But they seemed to be getting along, they seemed to have some kind of weird understanding, which is all the weirder considering how things turned out.

Eventually, I was called in to meet Holly. I marched slowly across our long rose-colored carpet, toward the two of them seated on the sofa like royalty or movie stars or something. Like I should have bowed or something.

"Well, here he is," Lila exclaimed flashing her broad, phony grin. "Jed, this is your new tutor, Mr. Flood."

"Good morning, Jed," Holly said.

I said, "Hi." I hated him.

Lila turned daintily toward Holly and wondered, "Wouldn't you like some more tea, or a scone, perhaps?"

Holly rose—he was so tall above me then, like a giant—and took his cane, which had been leaning against the glass and marble coffee table. "No, thank you, Mrs.

Levine. I think Jed and I had better get acquainted." Very soft spoken, direct. "Will you show me the way, Jed?"

I shrugged. "Yeah, sure, okay." So, I did hate him when I first met him. But, you know how people always say that adolescents are always acting out, trying to get attention by being bad and everything, but what they're really doing is crying for help? Well, I think there's a lot of truth to that. I did want to be helped, I really did. So, some little piece of my brain or heart or guts or whatever saw Holly as the answer to a prayer. Which I didn't even know I'd been praying. If that makes any sense.

Holly followed me up the front stairs, through the second-floor corridor, past the bedrooms and baths to the back of the house, down three steps into the room we called the solarium, a gigantic square room with floor-to-ceiling windows and a green tile floor. Lila had set it up for us to use as a schoolroom. There were a large wrought-iron and glass table for studying, a few walnut bookcases, a rolltop desk for Holly, and an antique school desk for me. Also, Lila's old hi-fi set was in there, and some scratched up classical music records. She had thrown in some other school-type stuff: a globe, a chalk board, pads of construction paper, and notebooks and pencils.

Holly looked around the place. "This will do just fine," he said. "What do *you* think, Jed?"

I didn't answer. I sat down at my desk and folded my hands.

Then Holly made this gesture, which I've now seen him do thousands of times, maybe millions: he puts the ring finger of his right hand onto the very outside corner of his left eye (if you can picture that; it's the weirdest kind of motion to make). Then rubs a tiny, delicate circle and sighs softly, like he's just exhausted. He blinks.

Holly had an unusual teaching method, his own sort of style, very vivid. He believed in concentrating on people rather than subjects. So, for example, we studied Emily Brontë, who wrote *Wuthering Heights.* So we read the book, of course, and then we read some stuff about Emily Brontë and her sisters and then some stuff about Victorian England and the history and all of that. And then it got extended—that's Holly's term; he always was saying, "Extend it, extend it, take it as far as you can." He can be really dramatic and everything. So, for example, we were reading about Catherine and Heathcliff and the moors and the heather and all of that and Holly asked me, "Do you know what heather is? Do you know what the moors are?" So, we got these books about the English countryside and vegetation and wildflowers. And every word we came across that I didn't know, we looked up and wrote down the definition. I remember I had never heard the word *morose* before, and if you've ever read *Wuthering Heights* you know there's actually quite a lot of morose in there. Some other words I remember even until this day—*hebdomadal,* which means *weekly,* and *moiety,* which means *portion.* Also, *interjacence, phlegmatic, catafalque, onus.*

Anyway, *Wuthering Heights* led Holly to start talking about narrative, different voices telling the story, and then about literature and authors who experimented with these weird sorts of techniques and how when movies got invented it changed how people related to reading and to stories. So from this one book, I got a whole education.

That's what happened with other people we studied, too. We listened to Duke Ellington and then read all about popular music and the recording industry and then racism and civil rights. It went on that way when we studied different painters, writers, musicians, scientists. One idea would lead to another, one book would lead to another.

There were some people Holly would not discuss. "Mark Twain is an utter bore. If you want to read Mark Twain, do it on your own time; the same with Gertrude Stein. These people are frauds." And he didn't know a thing about any music after about 1950 or so.

Holly had a rather complicated theory about what really matters and what really does not matter. It all seemed arbitrary to me, I never could figure his logic. Truth mattered to Holly. But also, he was so full of contradictions, and you just couldn't argue with him. I'd get frustrated, I'd see how he wasn't consistent, he wasn't fair. Kids really depend on things being fair.

"But, of course. That's the truth. People and things never *are* consistent, Jed. Life isn't *at all* fair." He looked at me like question marks were plastered on his wide, dark, kind of crazy eyeballs; and the question, always, was, Do you understand?

Holly

It is just three o'clock. Time to take one of my little pills. I keep them an absolute secret now. I pull one discreetly from my trousers pocket and pop it, with a child's grief and glee, into my mouth; swallow with a bit of water. In moments, a gorgeous sensation, profound, familiar, overtakes me. I really can never understand why drug addicts complain so bitterly, unless it is that they've not found the right drugs. For me, this action of taking one of my pills and the feeling that follows is always gratifying, always perfect. I love my pills; they are full of really concrete meaning, and that is such a rare thing. I don't care one bit about any danger drugs may represent. Intoxication is a natural part of life.

My little pills are the only gift I have to give myself. Perhaps that's sad, but isn't the world full of sad things?

Some soft, dreary piano music is being played over the speakers. Flanagan and his student friend are here still, across the room; a whispering little group has joined them. Flanagan glances with disdain around the café. A young woman approached their table and asked Flanagan to sign a battered hardcover copy of that wretched first novel of his—I think it was called *Dungeon View*—and he scribbled his name without once looking at her, in fact he kept chattering on to his spellbound companions.

One of Flanagan's books was titled *This Dusty Earth,* which is just stupid, it's hack; another was *Those Who Succumb.* And I come to realize how absolutely vital it is to me that I never seem pretentious. Understand—I certainly do not possess any less pretense than Flanagan; but his inability to hide this quality is a desperate, dreadful nightmare in my mind. Let me at least seem modest. It is practically my mission in life: to maintain an appearance of humility.

Upon our first meeting, Jed's contemptible, strident mother told me Jed was a genius. "He's gifted," she declared. As she scrutinized my *curriculum vitae* and reference letters—flawless but fraudulent documentation—she told me it was her belief that her boy's school troubles stemmed from his superior intelligence, that he was bored in his classes, his mind was being wasted. All parents think that—or say it, at any rate.

"What will be your focus with Jed, on what will your studies concentrate?" she asked and bit a caramel, offering a plate of candies to me, which I did not even acknowledge.

"What I want to teach your son," I answered—and I was taking such a risk—"is never to be sentimental, never to be rude, to trust his own instincts. How to live, Mrs. Levine. And, most of all, how to read."

Well, Jed's mother chewed on this bit of caramel, holding another piece aloft between her ring finger and thumb. She stared at me. Then she smiled broadly. "Oh, that's just *fascinating,* Mr. Flood," she cooed. I don't think she found it fascinating at all, I think she considered me preposterous (which I was). Jed's mother was completely false.

"I am in some ways quite conservative, Mrs. Levine," I went on. "History. Literature. The great philisophical questions. Art. My own education . . ." And as I elucidated an entirely fabricated classical training, Jed's mother blinked at me excitedly, as though she'd just found the right color drapes to go with the sofa.

What I want to teach your son, I might have said, is how to be true. How not to be like you.

So, Jed's a genius, Jed's gifted, but Jed's been associating with the wrong sort of people, Jed's been bored and depressed because Jed's a genius, he's gifted, and so forth. When she called the boy in to meet me, though, I did not see a genius at all. I saw a very complex, sad, mean little package.

I saw profound sorrow. A queer wisdom, too. Nothing sinister in the boy, nothing contrived. And sex all over—a perfectly winning little form. A splendid curve to his butt when he stood with his weight on his right leg; smooth, smooth brown arms and slender fingers; a dark complexion without blemishes or bristle; handsome lines to his cheeks, his jaw, his brow. A gentle roundness at the shoulders. At thirteen years old, he was a delicious, coy flirt. He was waiting—I do know that waiting look. Waiting to step forward into his life, to move. Waiting for me? I believed I had his number down.

His mother said, "Jed, stand up straight please, dar-

ling," and Jed smirked, an expression calculated to go
unnoticed by that dismal mother of his but to be seen and
fully understood by me, which it was.

Julius wipes his right eyebrow with the tips of two fingers,
purses his lips. "Oh, I went to see Nick in the hospital
yesterday. Have you gone?"
    I shake my head.
    "Well, he's not the same person, he's completely
unrecognizable. And nasty. I'll tell you one thing: just
because someone has AIDS doesn't mean they're pleasant
to be around. I guess it's just the most unfashionable thing
you can possibly do to criticize an AIDS victim, but I mean,
really, if you're just a snotty little shit, getting AIDS will
not change that. And we all know what a snotty little shit
Nick has always been.
    "I think, I really do think that Nick wears this AIDS
like a badge. Like, 'See, I got fucked, I shot up, I had *fun*
back in the good old days.' But, of course, the minute he
turned twenty-four years old no one wanted to have a
thing to do with him. He was so stupid. So, when that
dreamy little-boy look was gone, well, who needs him?
See, Holly, I mean, you were one of those pretty boys, but
you aged gracefully. Gracefully."
    "Thank you, Julius, thanks for that."
    "I had sex with Nick, you know."
    "I know." I barely remember Nick. Too pretty and
blond and muscular, not nearly boyish enough for my
tastes. But I do recall the messy drama of Julius and Nick's
short affair.
    "Oh, but it was years ago. He was unbelievably cruel
to me. He called me a pockmarked old queen and stole

every Valium in the house *and* gave me crabs, so I hunted him down at that horrible bar he used to hang around in and threw a bottle of lice medicine at his head, right there, right in front of everyone. Really, he's always been just the most despicable monster. Well, *you* know.''

"Yes, I know.''

"He was really in the most terrible denial, for *months.* He kept saying he thought he had the flu. Then, of course, that famous night when we all went to Patrick's perform-ance piece and Nick had diarrhea and was hopping up and down to the bathroom throughout the entire evening. And he had the nerve to say he thought he had a touch of food poisoning. Food poisoning, *really.*

"But—now he's dying. And everyone's just so shat-tered by the whole thing. Visiting him, holding his hand. Everyone wants to push him around in his wheelchair. Can you imagine what his funeral will be like—what lies people are going to have to make up just to be polite? You can't stand up at someone's funeral and say, well, he was really the cheapest little whore we've ever run across. No, no.

"God forbid they find a cure for AIDS tomorrow or something, Nick won't know what to do. He's practically built a career on being terminally ill.''

This remark of Julius's, naturally, kicks a trigger of my own. I feel the ancient cough in my throat, I feel shooting pains in my poor legs. I feel a burning sensation at my temples, dryness in my mouth. I feel the singular rum-blings of that mighty headache, the inherited ache, Mama's legacy. I feel sick. I am sick.

"Anyway,'' concludes this wretched Julius, "fags just love tragedy. It's a human truth.''

*   *   *

Summer mornings in our town were misty, gray, heart-sick, as though the sun was unwilling to show us any brilliance.

Aunt Joy liked to make my breakfast—cold cereal with bananas and orange juice. "You want some toast, sweetie?" I would nod. "Well, then let's make you some toast."

Aunt Joy had the radio on, and when a very favorite song came on she waltzed grandly across the scuffed black-and-white tile of our kitchen floor, singing along, turning, bending. As she held a slice of bread in each hand, Aunt Joy began to spin in a tiny circle. Her red hair had been tied in a knot and now it came undone, as Aunt Joy made her swift turns, at once awkward and graceful, and sang and laughed. "Look, look, look how my dress twirls . . ." she called out. Like a girl on a carousel, shouting each time her horse passed by me. I held tiny fingers to my red ears, smiling wide.

"Joy." Mama was suddenly in the kitchen. She pressed the knob on the radio, cutting off the music abruptly. "Joy, I thought you were going to be fixing Holly's breakfast, not performing your exotic dancing routines."

Aunt Joy laughed, turned, and placed the slices of bread in the toaster. "Well, good morning to you too, Faith."

Mama walked toward me, licked the ends of her fingers, and patted my stubborn cowlick saying, "Damn thing never stays down."

"We're having cereal and toast, Faith. You want something?"

"Coffee." Mama stepped over to the back screen door

and gazed out for a moment. "It's going to rain again today," she said.

Aunt Joy stood gazing at my mother. I looked at one then the other. Aunt Joy was slender, her posture childish and loose. Mama was facing away; her back was broad and square, stiff.

Aunt Joy said, finally, "Faith, aren't you going to be late getting to Asylum Street?"

There was a long, stale silence. "I can't go there," Mama whispered, but she did not turn around. "I don't think I can go back there."

Aunt Joy was quickly beside my mama, had her arms around her shoulders, her fingers firm as she guided her, turned her, led her from the room. "Let's get you dressed and cleaned up, Faith. You've got to go to work. You know you've got to go to work."

I stayed on the wooden chair at the kitchen table, swinging my bare legs, unable to comprehend anything but the undefined mood of urgency and that some precise strategy was being kept secret from me.

Something was wrong. Mama was sad. Aunt Joy was taking care of her. I was forgotten.

Childhood. The story of my childhood is a fable that has a center, a heart; it must have an ultimate moral. The story of my childhood has, too, a main character: delicious Aunt Joy.

Sitting on our weathered wicker chair on the porch, she would lift her shoulders in a sensual rocking rhythm to the jazz music from the radio inside. A cigarette stuck between her lips, her eyes closed. Jazz music on the radio took Aunt Joy away, to a world of her own, where she was oblivious of being observed, she was actually without cares. She was all sensation—unqualified, uninhibited, heedless feeling. And when a song would end, Aunt Joy sighed with deep, almost embarrassing contentment. Her sister, my mama, would shake her head disapprovingly at this and any other kind of display.

The thing to be remembered about Aunt Joy is how very much I admired her. That I wanted to be like her. She was a vision for me of what was possible when one was grown—a startling other vision than that which my own mother represented: one of fatigue, vague resentment, tension.

Aunt Joy loved soft, pinkish light. Her laugh, though small, not really forceful, was full of distant mischief. Aunt Joy always looked beautiful. No matter what she wore, how her hair was done, what her mood was, what her day had been like, regardless of the town's relentless dust or that dim light in our house, Aunt Joy shone.

Another thing Mama used to say of Aunt Joy: "She trusts the world."

More than the objects children long for, or the friends or attention, more than any conception of what might one day be in store for me in an adult world of love and work and travel, I wanted very much what my thrilling, beautiful Aunt Joy seemed to possess with inexplicable, defiant ease: to trust the world.

"But, anyway, darling," says Julius. "Listen. Where are you keeping that adorable little friend of yours? What was his name?"

"Jed," I reply.

"Jed. What a masculine little name that is, isn't it?" Julius leers, and I spin my empty coffee cup in a circle. "We all adored him so. Where is he these days?"

"I don't know, really. He said something about going up to San Francisco. I'm sure he's with a very competent psychiatrist, sorting everything out."

"Oh, I see." He draws deeply on his cigarette, exhales absently. "Children can be so cruel. Do you know why the chicken crossed the road?"

I do not answer.

"Well, to get to the other side, of course."

Jed

Everybody thinks, or they thought, or I guess they still think that Holly kidnapped me. It's sort of true, but it sort of isn't true.

You can always read in the papers about little kids who are abducted from parking lots or whatever and raped or kept in cages or whatever. On the sides of milk cartons they'll have these photographs sometimes of smiling little kids and it'll say HAVE YOU SEEN ME? Some little kid was innocently walking along on his way to school and then never came home or something. You can see interviews with these frantic, desperate parents, see them practically coming apart at the seams.

My mother was even interviewed on TV when this whole thing first happened. We watched it. The news guy pushes this big microphone in front of her and asks, "What would you like to say right now to your son's kidnapper, should he be listening?" So, Lila takes a deep breath, her

eyes get all wet. "Don't hurt my son. Don't hurt him. I'll
do anything, I'll pay any amount, whatever you want. Just
. . . please . . . don't . . . hurt . . . him." Then she kind
of shook her head, covered her eyes with her hand like she
was too overwrought to continue, she was apologizing to
the news guy.

Holly said, "What a performance." Which kind of
hurt my feelings a little bit. I mean, I wanted to think my
mother really was upset at my being kidnapped. A little
bit, anyway. "It's an act, Jed," Holly said.

But about this kidnapping—it's sort of true and sort of
not. It was winter, cold, dirty, and wet. Everything
smelled musty. Lila and her two best girlfriends from her
college days, Bea and Greta, had gone off for a couple of
weeks skiing, even though Lila had never been on skis in
her life. She bought an outrageous outfit for the trip,
though, the most expensive, the most fashionable kind of
winter wear. I thought she looked miserable stuffed into
this snowsuit, trying to stay chic. She left me and Holly
alone, except for the maid, Barbara. (Lila had eventually
caught Eliza stealing the silverplate candlesticks. Oh, Lila
was completely livid and everything. "Don't you 'thee'
and 'thou' *me,* young lady," she shrieked, her earrings
flapping. "You're fired!" So, then she went through about
fifteen more maids before she found Barbara, a very pleasant Jamaican woman, and Lila said, "Next time I hire a
deaf-mute, so I don't have to listen to a bunch of bullshit."
Holly thought this was very funny.)

Holly and I had been together a few months by this
time. He lived in an apartment in a modern building
outside of the town, miles from my house. He came every
morning at 7:30, rode in on the bus. I would watch out my
window as he walked from the corner; he'd be talking and

laughing with a couple of the maids who worked in our neighborhood, and Holly and the maids would wave good-bye to each other. I got the impression the maids liked Holly very much, actually.

Then Holly and I would have juice and toast. He read the paper. Then we would head upstairs to our school-room.

I was learning so much: definitions of words, different facts and ideas about art, history. (No math. Holly told me very early on that he didn't know a thing about mathematics and that we should just not tell my mother that fact.)

One whole day we spent studying the presidents of the United States. I learned about all these treaties, wars, different kinds of legislation, the electoral college, voting. How the candidates used to do their campaigns on trains. Also, in the old days, there were pigs and cows walking around Washington, D.C. And at the end of this day of learning about the presidents, Holly said, "So, if you really study history, Jed, you'll understand that things have changed very little and are hardly likely to. It's true in all of life. Now, that may give you either anguish or comfort."

How he spoke was the first thing to notice about Holly, actually. His grammar was perfect and so formal; he was meticulous when he spoke. He was like a gentleman in one of those old English novels. "I cannot fully enter the modern world," he told me. "I'm a dinosaur, perhaps. Socially, I have no boundaries, I'm an outlaw. But aesthetically, culturally, I'm an arch-conservative."

I wrote a lot, filled a couple of notebooks, in fact. I guess, actually, I did work rather hard, harder than I had in regular school. But the thing about being with Holly is that I never felt like a pupil, I never felt he was talking down to me, assigning things, demanding; he didn't seem like any kind of authority. In fact, we were both just busy with our little projects, just content. Holly did guide me somehow, I guess, but it felt natural. There was a job to be done—to learn about marine life, let's say—and then we'd both just start reading, listening to records, drawing pictures. We'd ask each other questions here and there, but we were very quiet much of the time too.

More than facts and dates and all of that, I was starting to think differently. To question things. Like, you know how they say the vowels are *A, E, I, O, U,* and sometimes *Y?* So, I asked Holly, "When? *When* is sometimes *Y* a vowel?" That's the kind of thing they tell you in school, but no one ever explains it, no one challenges it. And then I got on to wondering, "If we're taking photos of Mars, maybe Mars is taking photos of us."

"Well, we're not certain there are live beings on Mars," Holly explained.

"But, see, I mean, maybe on Mars they're saying the same thing about Earth. I mean, it *could* be, couldn't it?"

After a pause, Holly said, "Yes, yes, it could be." So, I know he really didn't think there were people on Mars or anything, but I know he loved that I was asking these questions, wondering about it, arguing about it. And he said, "I hope they have superior photographic equipment, Jed. I hope they get a good, clear photo of the two of us."

Somehow all this about Mars led Holly to talking about mythology. What was it?—now I can't even remember. Mythology and revolution or something. So, about the industrial revolution, the sexual revolution, political and military uprisings as expressions of the human search for myths and gods. Oh, and he said a whole lot about psychology: it represents the revolution of the individual, in contrast to the collectivity, and it destroys society and all of this is natural evolution or whatever. "There was Copernicus; then there was Freud." I tried to write down everything he said. But Holly always confused me. Sometimes it seemed like he was talking to himself, raving on with his theories. He was magnificent to watch, his passion; and a little spooky, too. In a weird way, actually, I loved it all, even being spooked.

Holly hated when I used the word 'weird,' which I did a lot, actually. He was correcting my grammar constantly—mostly when to use what word—and I still can never get it straight. *Who* or *whom, that* or *which, were* or *was*. I do have *me* and *I* pretty much figured out. Trying to improve my vocabulary frustrated Holly; he said teaching me proper English would be an entire year's project.

Another of Holly's special passions: he was always drumming into my head the evils of religion. "But I'll prove it to you historically," he said, "so you have facts at your disposal and won't get swayed by spiritual sentimentality." I don't remember much of what he had me read or his lectures. He presented the Spanish Inquisition in a fairly vivid way, actually, like he was telling a story; and his whole point was how much bloodshed and corruption occurs in the name of religion. "First the Moors took over Spain and ruled for eight hundred years or so. Then the Christians came and plopped their cathedrals and statues and all their other nonsense right on top of the Muslim mosques and drove out the Jews and the Moors." Holly was quite fired up about this subject. He seemed to have the most anger toward the Christians—telling me in detail all the wars, the atrocities—but I got the impression that, to Holly, pretty much any church or temple, etc., was dangerous, capable of destroying people and cultures in the name of their God. He spoke about it often, every day, actually. It was too complicated for me.

And then he would talk about right now, here in America. "The fundamentalists. It's the same impulse, you know, with these fundamentalists. People are so astounded that these crackpots turn their attention to politics; but the church has always been political, it's always sought power and fought to maintain and expand its control. That is its history. Organized religion demands intolerance."

I was probably yawning or fidgeting or something, because sometimes I just couldn't follow Holly's train of thought. "Anyway," I said, "don't you think it's okay if people just want to go to church?"

"If people want to go to church? Why would I possibly care what *people* want to do?"

See, Holly could be very cutting that way. It's an example, like I said before, of how Holly lacks compassion. He'd start a discussion and then, when I'd say something, just brush it off. "I don't know, Holly, I mean, people get comfort out of the stuff at church."

"Do you? Do you find church 'stuff' comforting?"

He seemed angry, and I found myself getting angry too. "Maybe not. But some people do, all right?"

"I imagine there were those who felt comforted by gaslight. Or horse and buggies. Or even walking on all fours. Jed, what you have to understand—and it's deeply painful—is that people are all instinct. Yes. People are motivated, as are all animals, by need—the need to survive. So, we identify what we need—it's sex, money, home, love, food, it's a million things for different people, Jed. And then they will do anything, they're capable of anything. So we require very intense, complex structures to direct us toward—well, not so much toward doing good, but away from doing what's thought of as bad.''

Here, I was almost afraid I was going to cry. Because Holly was too smart for me. No, not too smart; too quick, too sharp.

''Well, what about God, then?'' I asked him. ''I guess you don't believe in God or anything.''

Now, the thing is, I did not actually believe in God myself. Around eight years old I had figured out that God was just this story people told themselves. Everyone's afraid, and they know they have to suffer in life and go through diseases, tragedies, etc., and then they'll just die, of course. They can't accept it or whatever, so they go with this story about a life in the hereafter and God. And I knew Holly was talking about history, politics, kings and queens, and everything—not really about God—but he just was getting to me, his narrowness. Holly's a very narrow man. So, I threw out this question about believing in God, and I had no idea he'd have such a weird reaction.

He took a sudden, quick inhale. Then let it out and looked down and sort of played with his fingers, like he was an embarrassed little kid or something. ''God?'' A few minutes later, he lifted his head, looked at me again. ''Don't misunderstand me, Jed. I've been trying to teach you about the church. Religion—that's not about God, that's about man.'' He stood up, walked over to the windows that looked out over the wide lawns, the trimmed hedges, the garden. ''No person in his right mind can believe in God. Start with that. Then, you live a little bit, and you realize no person in his right mind can afford not to believe in God. Faith means survival.''

It's funny, but Holly's mother's name was Faith. I

think that's pretty ironic. I can't remember now what his aunt's name was—Hope or something like that. Anyway, I couldn't follow what he was saying exactly. The way he was sounding and moving was very dreamy, sad, kind of lost. No, the word is *melancholy*. I love that word.

He went on, "One resigns oneself. At first, one fights against stupid, cruel, destructive myths and the pain religion has caused, its deep flaws, its repressive forces; one rebels against the desperation in the human craving for meaning, which makes people greedy rather than searching. In youth, one rejects belief, mocks faith and worship. That is what youth is for. But, finally, one must be resigned. It—the world, life, suffering and joy, the human heart—is all just too big, overwhelming, too mysterious." Since he'd been looking at the garden, I guessed he was talking about nature. And I've had that thought, too: there must be a God, because just take a look at the flowers, ocean, mountains, sky, etc.

Then Holly turned and looked at me and said, "One day I woke up with the discouraging certainty that, in fact, *I* am *not* God. It was a terrible day."

So, I thought I knew what Holly meant, but then it seemed I didn't really know, I only partly understood. He said we were going to read Saint Thomas Aquinas. A little poem ran through my mind: Melancholy Holly. Why so melancholy, Holly?

That's when I thought I really might be in love with Holly, actually.

One day Holly and I were in our schoolroom making a mobile: different size branches with pieces of thin yarn hanging from them and buckeyes and little stones attached at the ends. We were studying space and time. We'd made a calendar. We'd drawn maps.

"I think we'll take the entire spring for a comprehensive study of evolution," Holly said. "We can't be at all cursory in our study of evolution. We must dig very deeply into the material—scientifically, but, more important, philosophically."

I unwrapped this little lemon sourball that I'd had in my pocket for about a year or something and I was sucking on it.

"If you're such a genius, Jed, you'll be up to a scholarly approach to evolution."

"I'm just a kid, don't forget," I said, and then we both laughed.

So we kept putting this mobile together, with paste and thumbtacks, etc. The whole trick of it would be the balancing. All of a sudden it turned kind of gray outside and then this slushy snow started, more like rain, actually. Holly got up and stretched his arms over his head. He put a Schumann record on; he said he played Schumann a lot because Schumann was so sad.

After a while Holly said, "I have to get out of here." He said it so softly I wasn't sure for a second if he had meant for me to hear.

"Out of here?" I asked. "You mean of this room? This house, you mean, or this town? Or what?"

"I have to move."

"Oh. To move."

"I have to travel."

"Oh. Travel. You have to see different things or something?"

"I'm trying to explain it to you, Jed. But I'm distracted."

"Don't you like it here anymore?"

"Anymore? I don't know that I've ever liked it here. That's an assumption. I don't know that I've ever——"

"I just thought——"

"I'm trying to say that I don't think I've ever really liked it anywhere."

"Oh, anywhere. . . . Where should we hang this mobile? By that window?"

I think I was nervous because of what Holly was saying. I do get nervous sometimes and then I tend to change the subject. I think I was afraid he was going to leave, or whatever, and I didn't want to take him too seriously. But he was serious. He stepped over to the window I had pointed out, stood there, just stood there and ran a finger along the sill.

"Holly? What about when you were little? What about your home?"

"Home. Home was very smoky and quiet and full of echoes. Home was a very sad place. But it was beautiful and strange. So since then I've always been searching for something sad and beautiful and strange."

"Do you miss your mother?" I don't even know why I asked that question. I just get nervous sometimes and ask weird questions.

"Do you miss *your* mother, Jed?" Holly said this rather harshly.

"Well, then, how about some exotic kind of place? How about Spain?"

"I've been to Spain."

"Morocco."

"I've been to Morocco."

"Well, there's all of Europe or Africa or China or whatever. There's a million places to go."

"Yes. I hate them all."

"Really?"

"In every place I feel alienated and outside and frightened. I feel threatened and vulnerable. The more foreign a place is, the more it does not belong to me and I am no part of it, the more dangerous it seems."

"Russia."

"I've been to Russia. Russia is depressing."

"Hey, how about Canada? Canada's close anyway."

"Canada is an extremely sinister environment."

"What do you mean? Why are you laughing?"

"Because . . . oh, just how ridiculous I can be."

"Holly? Who is Samuel Beckett?"

"A very brilliant, important playwright."

"I came across the name. Can we read some plays he did?"

Holly didn't answer. He seemed far away, not really thinking of something specific, not worried or upset or anything, just far away.

Then, again, he said he had to get out of here.

This melancholy Schumann music was going, and the snowy rain. I wanted to ask Holly about his mother and when he was a little boy, but I was afraid. And I was getting angry at him, too.

"Do you think running away will solve your problems?" I asked.

"I'm not interested in solving my problems." He turned away from the window and sat beside me. I couldn't look Holly in the eye for some reason, I kept fiddling with the string and sticks and one of the buckeyes rolled off the table, across the floor, under a bookcase.

"Hey," I said, all kind of excited, "how about America? You know? Why does it have to be some place so far

and everything? What about traveling all around America?''

The music stopped all of a sudden.

He said, ''Well, I think that's an excellent idea. And
I think we should start tomorrow morning. I think what I'll
do is book passage on a train. A train will be the most
pleasant and convenient, at least to begin with. Eventually,
I suppose, we'll want to rent a car. You have to make a list
of books to bring, though, and other supplies.'' He flipped
a page on a pad of paper in front of him and began making
notes. ''Clothes, of course. Toiletries. Plenty of sharp
pencils. A notebook. We might even be able to find a
portable typewriter to take along with us.''

So the kidnapping was like that, actually. It started out
Holly talking about himself, wanting to move, needing to
go away and me being sad and confused, mad at him—but
I hardly even knew what I was feeling. Then it was just
assumed somehow that I would go along with Holly. We
were not done with each other. It wasn't time for us to be
apart. I didn't understand all about Holly yet—about his
creepy, weird childhood and the crazy mother and the aunt
or anything. Or even why he had come in my life. But I
understood that we would be together.

I loved Holly. Everything that's happened since, anything people want to say or think about me and Holly, all
of how it looks or seems is irrelevant to me. I really loved
him. I *wanted* to be with him.

The papers said I was abducted. Holly pulled out
Roget's *Thesaurus* and had me look it up. ''Abduct, v. take
away, take off, run away with, kidnap, shanghai, carry off,
ravish (taking, thievery).''

''Now does *any* of that apply?'' he asked me. Which
it doesn't. I just followed after Holly. It was instinct

almost. Like if you are walking down the street and all of a sudden behind you is this friendly little pup and he starts following after you and he goes with you to your house. Then he looks hungry or something so you give him a little saucer of food. And he loves you and you keep saying, "Go on home now." But he doesn't want to go. Maybe he doesn't like his real home. He wants to stay with you. He curls up at your feet. He sleeps with you. And then it just seems like he belongs with you. You come to mean his survival. That's not exactly an abduction, is it? (Oh, but was I the little puppy, or was Holly?)

When we were on the train the next morning, it was just daylight, I was barely awake. I asked Holly, "Why is it, do you think, that you have to move around so much?"

"Because I'm lost."

"But if you're always coming and going, won't you just be even more lost?"

"Yes."

Holly

I can close my eyes. It is a special talent of mine. I can close my eyes here and shut out sound very quickly. It is something like dunking completely under the bath water, holding my breath, faithful that I will not drown, weightless and isolated; and then I am blind and hear only eerie, hollow echoes of my own motion in water. I can close my eyes, shut out all sound but hollow echoes; and this café and its patrons, Julius and Flanagan and the rest, all are magically gone.

In my life it is axiomatic that when I disengage in this curious way with the present—with now, with real life—I am instantly engaged again with the past—with then, with the dream life.

Ah, come around a shadowed bend. Walk all the way to where the pavement ends on Factory Street. Here is Asylum Street. Everything about it is crooked: the ancient, small stone fence on either side, the telephone poles planted along it, the trim of the hedges, the rocks scattered in the road. Asylum Street is uneven, disorganized. Near the hospital gate, rusting old cars and a truck or two are haphazardly parked on an ascending patch of brown grass.

The area has a low, confined feeling for the trees are never pruned, they are old and various; branches from several weeping willows sweep the ground and other trees spread, expand, creating a sheltered, dark path, and I cannot even see the sky.

I am very busy. I am walking down one side of Asylum Street, back up the other, concentrating so intensely on the manner of my steps: one foot directly in front of the other, heel to toe, as though I'm on a tightrope. This is not simply a game—it is a serious challenge.

In my left hand I hold the end of a wooden stick, a slightly curved, sturdy branch I have found. I let it drag behind me, describing a narrow line in the dust, bouncing gently over pebbles and twigs. It is marking my course.

I stop suddenly, kneel down with my knees on the gravel, resting my butt on the heels of my good shoes. This dusty line might be the road in a town. This large gray rock can be the town hall. These little stones are people's houses. These cracked, brown and gray rocks, covered with moss, set in a circle, these become the hospital where Mama works. All these pebbles are the crazy people in the hospital. They say nothing. They do not ever move. These twigs are the people of the town. They are walking to the town hall to have a meeting and the meeting is to decide if the town should have a big new highway running right through it. Half the people say yes, half say no.

I am biting my lower lip, for I am concentrating hard. There is no sound around me, only a vague tune in my head, a childish, rhyming lyric about my town and my people, the simplest kind of melody.

But something made me turn my head. All was still: the old stone fence, the telephone poles, the branches of the weeping willow. And suddenly there was Mama. She had been watching me. Her lips were light pink and dry, shaped in a smile, but it did not seem like a smile; her teeth showed and they were pale yellow. Her hair was not combed. Her arms were stiff at her sides, her fingers clutched and twisted the fabric of her dress. She looked crazy.

I cried out, jumped back from my toy town, lost my balance, and barely caught myself with my hands behind me. Mama stepped forward. "Oh, did I startle you, Hollis? Sorry, baby. I didn't mean to startle you."

I was breathless. I started to cry. Mama had turned, though; now she was a windblown white uniform and dark sweater and white shoes and white cap walking away, saying, "Come on, Hollis, baby. You got yourself all dirty. Mama's very tired. Mama's not feeling well. We're going home now, Hollis."

From *Death in Venice,* the novel Flanagan wishes he wrote—or, all right, the novel *I* wish he wrote:

True, what he felt was no more than a longing to travel; yet coming upon him with such suddenness and passion as to resemble a seizure, almost a hallucination. Desire projected itself visually: his fancy, not quite yet lulled since morning, imaged the marvels and terrors of the manifold earth. He saw.

At the beginning, I saw little of Jed's mother. Her interest in her son seemed cursory, mostly self-serving. She traveled often; she was highly respected for her charity work, quite capable, even bright, I suppose. But she was a wreck. I certainly know a wreck when I see one.

"What's your hurry, Mr. Flood?" she stopped me one morning as I was passing her open bedroom door. "Come in for a moment, come in, Mr. Flood."

"I was just taking some books up to Jed."

"How's he doing, anyway, Mr. Flood?" She'd put on her serious, concerned face and puffed her cigarette.

"Excellent, Mrs. Levine." By this time she had filed for divorce from her fourth husband.

"I *know* he's gifted." There was a breakfast tray on her bed and she grabbed a piece of toast, rather ferociously bit into it, and gulped some orange juice and exhaled smoke.

Lila never said one word about Jed that did not indicate her devotion, adoration, the most self-sacrificing and tolerant of attitudes. One might never have known that she despised her son.

She had taken to inviting me for late afternoon cocktails on the sun porch; by then she would already be a bit drunk.

"Well," said Lila, "I know how unbelievably difficult it must be for a boy in his position. Brilliant. Handsome. Popular. Oh, the other children look up to him. But he has no one." Here she leaned closer to me, holding her hands as though in prayer, the forefingers touching her lips. "No one, Mr. Flood." She clumsily sat back. "His father was a worthless shit. They look just alike, you know. And my career—I work very, very hard. I have enormous responsibilities, Mr. Flood. I'm the kind of woman who needs to be busy, to be contributing something. Sometimes I won-

der''—a wistful look at a corner of the carpet—''sometimes I wonder if I shouldn't have spent more time with
Jed.''

"I think not," I said. "I think he's had enough of
you."

"Thank you for that," said Lila, reaching out and
patting my hand.

My only reason for engaging in any conversation whatever with Jed's mother was to learn more about Jed—it
was not from any special interest in her. I have known
many other people like Jed's mother and resented them.

They are types; people, I imagine, who last felt truly
comfortable in their freshman college days, curled into a
corner of a secondhand sofa, smoking cigarettes, busy with
deep confidences among friends. They flourished in cozy,
protected smugness. After graduation, some entry-level
position, roommates in a walk-up, milk crates for book-
shelves. But not for long all of this deprivation and struggle, and it was never real anyway. Such people are meant
for success. They marry well, they move about. They are
never mistaken, never regretful, never caught, never lost.

I am not at all used to sexual advances from women
and, indeed, it's even been some time since I have been
advanced upon by a man. But I had a feeling regarding Jed's
mother—not that she was excited or attracted in any
conventional way, perhaps, but that she was curious about
me.

"So, you been married ever, Mr. Flood?"

"Excuse me?"

She was slurring her words shamelessly and she
laughed. "What I mean, what I mean is, is there a Mrs.
Flood?"

"No, I've never married."

With an ice cube in her mouth she grumbled, "Pity, that's a pity. You must date quite a bit? Attractive man like you?"

Well, in fact, I am not at all attractive. I've become, since my pretty-boy days, rather unappealing, perhaps in certain light actually frightening. So I did not answer her. I only looked at her sloppy half-grin and wondered what she could possibly want of me.

She had been reclining most inappropriately across a green wicker chair; suddenly she sat upright, smoothed her skirt, and held a hand to her breast. "Please forgive me if I'm getting too personal with you, Mr. Flood. Around here, we're all just family, sometimes I get . . ."

"Not at all, quite all right," said I.

The dynamics, if not the exact dialogue, of this scenario were enacted several times, out there on the glassed sun porch, under potted ferns. Jed's mother would give a little giggle, possessed, I thought, by some pathetic wish to go back to a time when giggling had come naturally, when it had suited her. She asked many questions about Jed: didn't I think he was a bit small for his age? and wasn't he so extraordinarily bright and talented? And questions about me, too: where had I traveled? where had I lived? whom had I known? When I told her I'd spent much of my youth in Los Angeles, she cooed and clapped, said how she adored Los Angeles.

My only question for her, and I did not ask it aloud, was: What is it you want?

It was astonishing to watch this woman construct our cozy friendship entirely on her own. I was less than encouraging, stony-faced and withdrawn, in fact.

She began inviting me for brandy or port after supper, just as I was getting ready to leave for the night. She reached her hand across the table toward me, wiggled her slender fingers. "Oh, please. Please. You must call me Lila. And I'll call you Holly?"

She was tireless on the subject of her husbands and, if she is to be believed, she really did end up at the hands of the most monstrous men: abusers, philanderers, thieves. One night, we had retired to the living room, a dark, gaudy mix of clashing furniture and colors, an hysterical blend of tastes and styles, which made it, finally, a disaster of a room. She had the maid light a fire. In the middle of her story about the man to whom she had been engaged who turned out already to have a wife and child (a story I'd heard before, incidentally), Jed's mother abruptly stopped speaking. She lowered her wine glass, splashing a bit onto the knee of her nylon. She stubbed out her cigarette. She gazed directly at me; I thought I must have some food at the corner of my mouth.

"Holly. Can I ask you a question?"

"Certainly."

"Holly—no, forget it." She turned her head.

Was I supposed to be encouraging, to insist? I really loathed Jed's mother.

She lifted her eyes toward a spot on the ceiling then and spoke breathlessly. "I feel so strange, Holly, I feel a little bit crazy I guess. I know I shouldn't ask this question, I shouldn't, but I can't help myself."

I thought suddenly that I must have Jed read Edith Wharton.

Jed's mother looked again at me, forcefully. "Holly?" She was so obviously loaded, I feared she would either sob or get mean.

"Yes, Lila?"

"Do you . . . do you . . . do you like me?"

Oh, people sometimes ask to be insulted, they dare one to betray. I shifted my glass in my hand, the ice cubes clicked dully. I was silent for several moments and kept my eyes down. I felt dangerous. Finally, I said: "Actually, I like Jed."

I had been Jed's teacher for almost four months. It was early winter. I was just beginning to suffer from my headaches: a subtle, dull pain on the top of my head, tender to the touch, a mild throbbing, which would cease as suddenly and inexplicably as it had come. I was growing weaker, too. My sleep was troubled.

So I knew something was terribly wrong, but naming this disease, charting or predicting its progress was quite impossible. I've always been afflicted. There was some sickness I'd had all my life, and if its symptom now was a constant headache, or sleeplessness, stiffness, paralysis, or anaemia, or boils, or hair loss it was all just a part of the greater illness I'd always known. Now, each morning I was tormented by a relentless hacking cough, which left me gasping, red in the face, teary-eyed.

(Not incidentally, this particular cough is a familiar and profound sound, it represents an entire context. When I was a kid, roaming through the city streets looking for dope, I'd often go with some older man to one of those shitty by-the-hour hotels. The man would get drunk. I'd let him do whatever he wanted. I always knew how pathetic these men were. I played tough, thought I was smart; and I was smart, I suppose. Then I'd get drunk or stoned and fall asleep and just before daylight, I'd awaken to that sound, that cough: deep, desperate, tragic, coming from some other room in the hotel, or from the building next door, somewhere above or below me, slapping its echoes against the bricks, bellowing through the air shafts and vents. I'd wonder: Can someone be dying, right now, dying? I'd grab my clothes and race out of the room when I heard the coughing. Now, of course, I have that very same cough myself.)

Jed was many things to me at this time in my life. He was my charge, my ward, my pupil, my job. But at this time in my life, getting weaker, I saw myself turning into a sad old character (sadder and older than Jed could comprehend). And for me, whose hearing was so poor, Jed was a sweet flute sound. Jed was the highest, most mellow note a flute can make. Jed was a soft rustling of leaves in a breeze. Jed was the coolest, calmest river.

One freezing, dark afternoon we were fiddling with yarn and sticks to make a mobile. I don't think Jed noticed me watching him, or at least he seemed oblivious to my intensity. He had been working with the mobile and took a moment to stretch his arms, to lean his head back.

I stared at his smooth, slender, almost copper-colored throat. Then he put both hands on his ribs and, stretching, rubbed his chest. His eyes were closed. It was an unfettered, immodest motion. One of his hands passed over the breast pocket of his plaid shirt and he seemed to feel something inside. He removed a tiny object from the pocket and held it in the palm of his hand. It was a gold-yellow, round candy, wrapped in clear cellophane, twisted at the ends. Jed examined this candy quickly but thoughtfully. He pulled off the paper. He blew a short breath on the sticky candy to rid it of dust or lint and before popping it into his mouth, shrugged his shoulders. It was the shrug that fascinated me—thrilled me, really. He considered himself unobserved, so his gesture was not for my benefit. He contemplated the candy—How old is this thing, where's it been, is it safe to eat it? Then, as children do—anyway, as Jed does—he discarded all worry in an instant and just tossed the little lemon ball into his mouth. He rolled it from side to side, where it formed a noticeable, bouncing bulge in his cheeks. I could hear it click against his teeth. Eventually, the moment came for the hard, profound bite, and I heard the candy crackle into pieces in his mouth.

Jed was sensuality. Jed was a boy stripping off his clothes and diving into a chilly, dark green spot of a river, rising up in a splash to shake his hair. I closed my eyes. I was thinking of spring. I was imagining naked Jed, diving, laughing.

One thing I dearly wished I could teach Jed was how to follow through, to complete what he begins. But you can't teach what you don't know. I don't know math, either.

I opened my eyes. "I have to get out of here." I said this suddenly, without thinking. "I have to move, I have to travel," I was trying to explain.

Jed asked, "Don't you like it here anymore?"

"I don't think I've ever really liked it anywhere," was my answer, but that was a lie.

Jed began to ask questions, jabbing them at me; it almost seemed he was hostile. I had one of my headaches, I was impatient.

"Do you think running away will solve your problems?" Jed asked.

I told Jed I had no interest in solving my problems, but I was thinking: No, no, maybe not, but running away might solve *your* problems.

*   *   *

In our neighborhood was a mangy dog, about knee-height, black and tan with huge, soulful, worried brown eyes and happy, alert ears. I wished he could be my dog. Mama did not like pets.

I wished he could be my dog, so I pretended he was. I would call to him. I named him Billy Jones. When I stepped out our back door, I would see Billy Jones idly strolling along the side of the road, carelessly sniffing and snorting. I'd whistle. His head would snap around, and then he would canter to me. Billy Jones liked me. It was as though he belonged to me. I'd say, "Here's my dog, *here's* my dog."

"Billy Jones? Well, that's a very good name for a dog, Holly," Aunt Joy said.

"I wish I could have my very own dog like Billy Jones though," I confided.

"Well, you know, people don't really own their pets. Nobody can own somebody else, even a dog. People just take care of them and love them. So, when you're playing with Billy Jones, that's enough."

One dry, blisteringly hot summer day I had taken a kitchen knife and was scratching my initials into the bark of a tree in our front yard. The world was motionless, soundless. I wore overalls with no shirt, my feet were bare. I had popped the green lenses out of a pair of Aunt Joy's plastic sunglasses. I was pretending I needed spectacles. I wished I did.

From somewhere behind me, from behind our house, I heard: "No!" It was Aunt Joy. "No, no, don't."

I did not run. I walked slowly, cautiously, peering through my pretend specs, holding my knife, and I reached the corner of our house, pressed myself against the wooden shingles, hugged the house, pulled myself around to see.

"No, don't!" I could only see the back of Aunt Joy, her red hair dazzling in the hard sunlight. Her arms were raised, her hands were in fists by her ears. She was looking down at Mama. Mama was on her knees. She was propelled by a strange, violent motion—her body lifting up, bearing down, up and down in a rhythm. I could not discern what Mama was doing. I squinted through my eyeglasses.

Aunt Joy turned in a half-circle, bringing her fists to her mouth. "God, Faith, what are you doing?"

I had a clear view of Mama then. She held her old umbrella, closed, with both hands. She was raising it high above her head and bringing it down hard against the ribs of Billy Jones, who was silent and still and staring with his worried eyes and waiting, I suppose, for me. Again and again she struck Billy Jones, and the sound was thick, hollow. Her neat hair had come undone and was damp with sweat, whipping her cheeks and throat as she moved.

"You'll kill that dog, Faith, what are you doing?" Aunt Joy cried out. I stepped from behind the house, moved closer. Then Aunt Joy and I both were saying, "No, stop. No, stop," she bellowing, angry, I high-pitched, frightened. And then our pleas merged, we were one insistent but powerless voice.

Mama collapsed. She dropped the umbrella. She put her hands to her face with the fingers spread, like she was about to scratch herself. I began to sob, but I did not move. Billy Jones darted, sped away, never looked back, never came back.

"Mama?"

"Faith, honey, my God. Faith, come inside. My

God.'' Aunt Joy took her sister by the elbows, led her through our miserable, tiny yard to the house and inside, and I stood alone there, furious tears streaming, my eyeglasses slipping down my nose.

Julius continues, ''Well, I guess, why not, I'll have one more drink. So listen, I saw Caroline yesterday. She's been out of the country. She was telling me all about her illegal abortions. She's had eight of them, you know. Abortion is a big bore if you ask me. I was saying, 'Well, Christ, Caroline, I mean it *is* murder. I mean, *really,* darling.' Now there are plenty of perfectly legitimate reasons for it and all of that, but we might as well call a spade a spade. I mean, I absolutely agree it should be legal and everything, I really do. But there are all kinds of legalized murdering. Killing in self-defense. Killing criminals in the electric chair. Darling, *war* is just mass murder, and *that's* certainly legal. But Caroline is very sensitive if you call abortion murder. She says 'terminating a pregnancy.' Well, to me that's like calling cancer a bad cold.

''Caroline is a very loathsome creature anyway, isn't she? Do I care if she's had abortions? I'm completely convinced that having this revolting messy blob of tissue mess inside you—if you're just really *opposed* to the whole thing—well, it's perfectly fine to have it disposed of. Before it causes any *more* trouble. Before it needs braces. Before it starts talking back. I support any woman who feels the need to murder her child—born or unborn. Do I care? Do I care?''

Jed

On the plane, Holly and I noticed a woman—young, in her early twenties—go into the lavatory. She was wearing a thick sweater and a long gray overcoat. We both just happened to notice her. The lighted sign clicked to OCCU-PIED. And then she never came out. After five minutes or so, I said to Holly, "Did you see that woman go in the lavatory? She's been in there so long." A couple of people stood outside the door, waiting to get in, and because the door never opened they headed off for some other lavatory.

Another ten minutes went by. "Hey, Holly, she's still in there, the sign still says 'Occupied.' "

"Occupied, occupied," Holly said, leaning back his head, closing his eyes. "That's so true, isn't it? The word resonates . . ."

"No, but really. Maybe she passed out or something."

He didn't open his eyes, he didn't move his head. He

only did that weird thing he does, putting his ring finger near the corner of his eye. "I'll tell you what happened. That young woman is pregnant. She began to feel herself going into labor. Well, she's unmarried. She's poor. She's frightened, virtually alone in the world. She's depressed."

"You're kidding around, but this could be something serious."

Then Holly looked right at me. "I'm not kidding at all. I know motherhood when I see it. She felt herself going into labor so she went into that lavatory and she's giving birth right this second. Then she will dispose of her fetus in the garbage can. Then she will return to her seat."

"You *are* kidding," I said, but I wasn't sure.

"I wouldn't kid about something so tragic and sick."

"But it's impossible."

"No. Happens all the time."

Holly put his head back again. I just kept staring at the OCCUPIED sign. This young woman was in there a half hour before she finally came out. A bald fat guy had been waiting for the lavatory and he gave her a dirty look. She walked down the aisle, right past us. She was holding her arms around her stomach. Her face was red and sweaty and the ends of her hair were stringy and damp.

Holly told me to watch the news the next day and I'd see a story about an abandoned baby on an airplane. I was quite confused and frustrated, actually. I almost believed Holly; but I *couldn't* really believe him. So, I never did watch the news. See, if it was really true or it really wasn't true—I didn't want to know.

I remember this weekend, right before Holly came to be my tutor. Lila and I went out to the country to spend a few days at this estate of her snooty friends the Thistles. She was very impressed by them because they were so rich and everything and they were on a lot of different committees and boards of charities or whatever. On the way, in the car, Lila was telling me how to behave with the Thistles, to be respectful and all of that, to have good table manners. And when we got there, she and the Thistles and this weird man friend of theirs who didn't say anything at all, sat around the dining room table playing bridge. The dining room was dark, the walls and furniture were mahogany, and there was a grimy brass chandelier with little yellow lampshades. The whole scene, actually, was very creepy. I think they just played bridge as an excuse to drink; they sure downed plenty of cocktails. Lila lied through her teeth, saying how well I was doing in school, and the Thistles and their weird friend kind of grimaced at me, like, Isn't that nice?

So, I spent most of the weekend in the Thistles' library room, reading these expensive photography books they had. And I kept getting excited at the idea of masturbating in this library room with all of them out there, so close to me, smashed, trumping and no trumping, or whatever. I thought it was funny and thrilling. The fact that one of them could walk in any second was, to me, pretty erotic or whatever. But I was too afraid and also thinking that Lila herself might walk in—well, that made me feel weirdly sick.

But there was a guy I kept seeing around, who was supposed to be working there, painting the garage. I never saw him do any work. He had a ladder propped against the garage, paint cans and brushes and stuff laid out. He wore white overalls and a T-shirt and a little painter's cap; he had pretty firm muscles, he was pretty handsome and everything. He kept wiping his forehead, like he was so tired from working so hard, but actually, it seemed like he spent all of his time smoking cigarettes, flipping through magazines, playing his radio. At one point, I was in the guest room where the Thistles had put me and through the window I saw my mother walking from the garden, past the garage. She stopped and told this painter guy to turn his radio off. He told her he needed it to work. ''I don't see you doing much work,'' Lila said. She had such nerve. So the painter said, ''Well, who are you, anyway?'' Lila said, ''Who am *I*? Someone who can have you fired in one minute, that's who I am. Now turn off that radio. It's giving me a headache.'' That's how she was. It was like she was always right about things and everyone else was always wrong. So the radio got turned off.

Anyway though, the point is that I got really obsessed with having this painter guy see me masturbate. I had this whole weird fantasy, which is a little embarrassing now when I think about it. I imagined standing in the window, off to the side a little, and with the curtain kind of covering me. The guest room had these sheer white curtains with little holes in them. So, I'd stand just near enough to the window to be seen from the garage below and I'd start to get myself hard and everything. This painter would be swigging from his can of soda and suddenly he'd catch a glimpse of me up there; he'd squint, he'd keep watching. I'd step a little closer to the window. I'd kind of push the curtain away and really be in full view and the painter would be really watching now, staring at me. Then he'd put his hand on his pants, begin to rub himself. Well, that's as far as this scene played out in my mind.

Through that day I became, I guess you'd say, quite neurotic and everything about my fantasy; I kept seeing it over and over, planning it out. I kept watching this dumb, lazy, muscley painter hanging around outside. And I really wanted this kind of sexual thing with him, this exchange, but from a distance.

Finally, late afternoon, I did it. I took all my clothes off and stood in the window and kept my eyes on the painter and stroked myself, keeping watch on the top of his head. I was wishing he'd look up. But I was shaking, too, because I guess I would have felt pretty surprised, shocked, embarrassed, etc., if he really did.

Well, anyway, he didn't look up. In fact, I kind of spurted all over the windowsill just as the painter was walking around behind the garage, disappearing. Then I felt dumb. I felt like sort of a little bit perverted or something for wanting this painter to see me naked and masturbating. I thought it probably wasn't normal. But, Holly said it isn't at all an abnormal impulse. "Everyone wants to be visible, Jed. It's just your way of trying to be seen." Which I didn't really get.

Of course, I have told Holly about these fantasies or whatever, we've talked about it a lot, actually. But it's so hard to explain, the real, real feeling—how it's kind of out of control and dangerous, but it's also quite exciting and everything. So, I stammered trying to get it all out and Holly said, "For such an articulate boy, you're really so inarticulate."

We landed at 6:00 A.M. or so at the Los Angeles airport. We'd been through so much already, Holly and I. And then the absolute most weirdest thing happened.

We had to ride this whole series of escalators and walk along these wide marble floors. Everything was so huge, surrounded by giant windows, and outside we could see the airplanes maneuvering, red lights on the tails and wings blinking in the darkness. The airport was silent, almost. Maybe my ears were just stuffed up.

So we were standing on this escalator. There was a woman in front of us and she started to cough. It was just a little tickly cough, but it was rather persistent. And Holly and I were tired, we weren't really paying much attention. So there was this couple behind us, a man and a woman, on the escalator, and suddenly they started coughing, too. I really didn't notice it right then, I mean it was just some people coughing. But as the escalator rose and met the next floor level I looked across this really brightly lit, enormous room and there were people whisking around, practically running, and everyone was coughing! People had handker-chiefs to their mouths and they were dragging their ex-hausted little kids and the kids were coughing, too. Even those red cap guys were coughing.

I looked at Holly and he was looking at me. Neither of *us* was coughing. Just then, we stepped off the escalator and it was like a scene of a plague or a war, chaos and confusion, all underscored by this coughing, this booming, hacking noise from every direction.

So I started laughing. I mean this just seemed, I don't know, this just seemed like the most absurd thing in the world, I got kind of crazily hysterical, actually. But when I looked at Holly, he had this spooky expression on his face, terror or something. His eyes were red, his lips were apart and whitish. It was like his skin had been stripped off him. He grabbed my arm. He kind of bunched the sleeve of my coat in his fingers. I stopped laughing then.

I felt very tender toward him. I hadn't ever seen him so scared. I hadn't ever seen anyone so scared, actually, not in such a sudden way, so fragile. I'd never seen an adult seem so much like a child.

"We're being gassed," he whispered, and squeezed my sleeve tighter.

I smiled. I guess like an adult would smile to calm down a worried kid. "No, it's okay," I said. "Let's scoot out of here. Cover your mouth and nose, follow me," I said, and we headed toward the electric doors.

Finally, some guy did come on the loudspeaker and make an announcement that somehow some stupid chemical had got into the cooling system of the airport and it wasn't dangerous or anything, but that's why people were coughing and it would be cleared up or whatever. I thought it was pretty funny because even this guy making the announcement was coughing after every few words. Holly never did think any of it was funny.

One thing to understand about Holly—and this took me some time, actually—is this idea he has about omens. He has a code.

Whenever we were driving, Holly would tell me to watch the signs. So I'd point out one for lodging or food or however many miles to such and such a town. And in this weird kind of way, for Holly the sign somehow said more than it said. "Sign—to signify. Think about that, Jed."

We took the narrow, badly paved back highways all through America. We left in early winter and as we traveled, the seasons changed, but Holly always moved toward warmth—first south, then west. America is lots of fields, lots of farms and factories. Then there is dust, then mountains. We didn't stop anywhere for too long. When we'd hit a big city, Holly would turn in our rental car for a different one. He never explained why we needed to switch cars.

Another thing he never explained—and I asked, actu-

ally, several times—was where he got all the money. He
had stacks of bills wrapped in socks in his suitcase. Every
few days he'd peel two or three of these bills from a bundle
and put them in his shirt pocket. He paid for everything in
cash.

Our destination was Los Angeles. "I know my way
around there," Holly said, and I knew he had friends there
and business dealings. But we didn't seem to have a time
frame or route or schedule. In fact, when we were in
Oklahoma, Holly saw an ad for a series of those old silent
Charlie Chaplin films playing at a college in Texas, so we
drove down there, got a hotel room, and stayed four days
just to see these movies, which I thought were pretty
stupid. Holly was trying to tell me all about the art of film,
the use of montage, all this sort of philosophical stuff about
the twentieth-century perspective and everything. I mean,
I thought the guy was funny, twirling around his little cane.
But actually it wasn't so deep. Holly always tries to make
everything so deep.

Anyway, one evening, just at sunset, we were sitting
on the hood of our rented car, eating egg salad sandwiches
left over from the day before. This was Iowa. The road was
one long line each way, straight, divided by a fading yellow
stripe. Everything there was flat. There were fields of corn
far off. There was no breeze or anything, but the air felt
damp.

So we hadn't seen any other people or cars for hours
by this time and we'd stopped to eat these egg salad
sandwiches. I was tired. I thought Holly was in a fairly
pleasant, easygoing kind of mood, actually. Sometimes he
could be like that. He was talking about finding a library—
he wanted us to look through the microfilm of old newspapers so I could learn about the history of Iowa or

something. He lit a cigarette and the smoke made a gray circle around his head. His face was so pretty in that greenish-silver morning light.

I said, "Hey, look, Holly. A car. That's the first car we've seen for hours."

Holly didn't answer me. We just watched this car coming toward us from the north. It passed by us with a huge whooshing noise, like a rocket taking off. And then we watched the back of it, going off down this straight road, south. The car was a bright red Volkswagen bug.

So then, about two minutes later I happened to look up again. "Well, I'll be damned," I said. "Look, Holly. Look at that." From the north, a red speck in the distance, coming closer fast, whooshing past us again, traveling south, disappearing. This car, too, was a bright red VW bug!

I said, "That's some coincidence, huh? We don't see any cars or anything for all this time and then two of the same kind of car pass us in a minute. That's really something, isn't it?"

"We have to go," said Holly. He hopped off the car and sort of scrambled into the front seat. He started the engine before I was even inside and sped off, squealing the tires. He kept both hands on the steering wheel. He was kind of grinding his teeth. He told me not to play the radio. He didn't talk to me for quite a while.

You shouldn't put shoes on a table. You shouldn't put a hat on a bed. Never look a dog right in the eye. No black cats, no walking under ladders. These things all mean bad luck. If two people say the same thing at the same time, that's a bad omen. Letting a candle burn all the way out is a bad omen. Churches, twins, nuns, and the police are all bad omens.

He said midgets were a sign of bad luck, too, and I said I really liked midgets, I really thought they were cute and anyway, they were just people, they couldn't help it that they had some weird deformity or whatever.

Holly said, "Well, stay the hell away from them."

Now I think of it, I don't remember Holly saying anything that meant good luck.

Holly

Kansas. It resonates. The middle of the nation, of these United States. The prairie, the frontier. Death and wind.

Kansas stinks of compromise. Its cities are not fantastic or beautiful or dramatic—they merely function, they work. Its small towns are far from each other, spooky and mean. Wind whips the straight highways and flat fields as though to punish the people.

If there is such a thing as a past life, and I am unfortunate enough to have had one, I know it was spent in Kansas—in the late nineteenth century, on an isolated, weather-beaten farm, the poorest kind of place. My mother and father were strong-bodied, ugly; they suffered separately and together. There was a shriveled granny in a corner rocking chair, mending the family's clothes, complaining of pains. I had big, dumb, dull brothers and sisters who worked in the fields and could not read. I was the baby. I died at two years old.

As we drove, Jed was restless—I'd forgotten how restless boys are and how irritating that can be for the grown-ups. Jed said, "God, it feels like we're in the middle of *nowhere.*"

"Nowhere? What does that mean?"

"You know what I mean. It's just a figure of speech."

"Well, perhaps you should think about your figures of speech carefully, so you know what it is you're saying." I would criticize Jed often in this ridiculous, teacherly manner, as though that were somehow my job.

"I *do* know what I'm saying. I'm saying it feels like we're in the middle of nowhere."

We had been south, then way up north, then a bit south again, according to no plan, only intuition. Now we were headed west along a narrow, twisting road, surrounded by pale, flat farmland. I had Jed read aloud to pass the time. E. M. Forster's *Howards End,* I think. But soon it grew dark, and there were no streetlamps, only a muted moonlight.

Finally, we saw a lighted sign alongside the road, a weathered painted billboard which read: DO NOT MISS THE LAKEVIEW LODGE AND RESTAURANT—JUST 20 MILES. There followed a series of similar billboards with various messages concerning this Lakeview Lodge and Restaurant, establishing almost a narrative flow: YOU ARE ONLY 18 MILES FROM LAKEVIEW! and DON'T MISS LAKEVIEW! and 10 MILES 'TIL LAKEVIEW! and other such signs. Somehow a promise was formed by this advertising, of something more than food and lodging. Weary travelers were being offered shelter, nurture, warmth, safety. Indeed, we were led almost to expect a version of Home. YOU ARE 100 YARDS FROM THE LAKEVIEW LODGE!, and as we turned onto its gravel drive I saw ahead of us, sure enough, a sign meant for those fools who would keep going, which read, OOPS! YOU JUST PASSED LAKEVIEW—DON'T YOU WANT TO TURN BACK?

This particular message filled me with apprehension and vague mistrust. I read too much into signs, I suppose.

It was already dark when we checked into our room, which was really a sort of cottage, attached to other cottages. We parked our wretched rented car right in front of the door.

The bed was not firm, and a worn pinkish spread was tucked over it. The walls were paneled with maroon-colored imitation pine, with little black knotholes arranged in a pattern, and the bureau and desk were the same. Around the room were hung cheaply framed drawings of kittens and cats with balls of yarn, peeking out of baskets, sitting on window ledges. One shaded lamp cast a weak, golden glow; the room seemed smoky.

Jed and I each had a suitcase with clothing and personal things, and we had an extra bag with our books and school supplies. We never fully unpacked because we did not stay in one place more than a night or two. This night we were both exhausted; we'd driven nine hours and had been bickering about a hundred little things—the map getting torn, when to stop for supper, if one of the tires felt low. Also, Jed had been pestering me since Ohio to let him drive. My argument was that he was not licensed, he was not old enough; his argument was that I was his teacher and here was a perfect opportunity for me to teach and him to learn and, anyway, wouldn't I get tired doing all the driving? Our relationship had evolved during our weeks of travel, creating a sense of a constant contest, a battle—nothing hostile at all, not resentment or bitterness. More, a dynamic of challenge. We fought not like boxers but like wrestlers: pushing, testing strengths and weaknesses, straining and then releasing. There was between us an unspoken knowledge, which is a beautiful but terrifying thing. We knew we would be together for quite some time.

I took off only my shoes and stretched out on the bed, more exhausted than I'd realized. Jed stepped inside the tiny, green-tiled bathroom and turned on the light switch, which cast a cone of yellow over the threshold. "God, it's like this bathroom hasn't been cleaned in a hundred years or something," he said.

I could see Jed at the sink, leaning forward to examine his face in the mirror—searching for whiskers? Blemishes? Or perhaps boys simply need to check themselves periodically, to see what they look like and if they have changed. "I feel gross. I feel completely grimy," he said, and took his clothes off, tossed them in a pile on the floor. He stretched his arm behind the shower curtain and, out of my view, turned on the faucets and then disappeared into the rush of water. That sound of water against the porcelain tub floor could have been rain on the tin roof of the shabby little house where I grew up. Jed was humming. Jed does not carry a tune at all well.

So, music. We will study more music. Folk songs. Broadway musicals. We can try some sensory exercises: What color comes to mind when you listen to a Bach violin concerto? Describe a scene or tell a story to Beethoven's Third Symphony. Close your eyes, Jed, and make up a melody. (We're in a field. Grass, with tiny yellow weeds, and in the distance is the perfect line of a cream-colored wheat field. Where is my cane? Jed is sitting, leaning back on his elbows, his legs stretched out before him. I am behind Jed, standing. I see him pick a blade of grass and bring it to his mouth. I want to see Jed's face and so I walk slowly around him. I see his jaw and a bit of his hair fallen across his brow. I say something about the Civil War. I want to teach Jed about the Civil War, and I start to talk about the North, the South, Lincoln. But Jed does not turn to me. I cannot see his face. I am afraid. I hurry around before him. I cough. Jed begins to laugh at me. Jed is laughing at me and I am coughing.)

"Holly? Holly?"

I heard his voice, felt his hand on my shoulder. I even knew it was he, standing over me; I knew where we were, that it was dark. But I started wildly, crying out, sitting straight up and rigid on the bed, holding my fists tight against my chest.

"Holly?" He sat beside me. He was still damp from the shower. He held the towel on his lap. "Are you okay? You had a bad dream or something?"

I shook my head but said nothing.

"Well, you sure got scared, you yelled and everything. You must have been having a nightmare."

I did not answer Jed. I put my hands to my face.

Jed put his arm around my shoulder, squeezed with his small, still-wet hand. "Hey. Hey, Holly. You're okay, Holly. You must have been dreaming." He put a finger under my chin, to lift my lowered head, to see if I was crying.

He whispered a soft, but strong, incantation: "Hey. Hey, hey. Hey. It's all right." Jed was stroking the back of my head.

Now the only light in this wooden little room came from the blinking orange hotel sign outside and from the moon. We laid back on the bed, then turned on our sides, facing each other. I still was wearing my clothes, Jed was naked. He touched my hair, my arm, my neck. This touch-ing, initially, seemed not to have any specific sexual in-tent—it was a sweet, clumsy tenderness. Jed sincerely wanted to make me feel better.

After some moments, I began to sniffle, to wipe the wetness from my eyes with my knuckle, and then I laughed. Jed laughed, too.

"You must have been having some bad dream, Holly," he said.

"No. I wasn't having any dream."

"Why did you wake up like that, though, shouting out and then crying and everything?"

"You have to have a reason for things don't you, Jed?"

Jed did not reply. He moved away from me, settled on his back. His body was a long silver shadow and a stripe of orange flashed across his face.

I do not think Jed could see me. Hidden there in the darkness, I said, "Jed, I think I called out . . . and why I cried . . . was because I *wanted* you to comfort me."

"And I did comfort you."

"Yes. You did."

There followed such long moments—time was wholly inaccurate, irresponsible. We laid together on this saggy bed, quiet. I did not know if Jed was asleep or not; and even when I felt sure he was, I thought he might be faking. Jed is a good faker.

Me, too, of course. I fell into and out of real sleep and the pretense. There would be a dream image of a frozen pond or of Aunt Joy riding her bicycle—and then I'd be back in the soundless, stale room, darkness the color of olives, listening for breathing. I'd grunt and sigh in my phony sound sleep, then wiggle around so that I was a half inch closer to Jed, a minute or hour closer.

Jed did not roll over or change his position at all. He did move, though. His dick was not fully erect, but let's say, it was aware: it was hard enough to show its pretty, perfect shape, its length, and with Jed's breathing (with his dreaming), it rolled against his leg. Once or twice Jed sleepily reached down and stroked himself, lightly, carelessly.

This night was a fast, silent movie, the mood changing every few moments, from excitement and suspense to stillness, lost dreaminess—and somehow Jed was like any beautiful boy on a screen, a flatness, a projected form; not a person but a character, a construction of shadow and light that cannot actually be touched but looks so real.

But maybe Jed will reach out to me now. I will put my hand on his chest, he'll turn. It was the drama of opportunity.

I wonder if I am sickly and crippled all the time because I am afraid to be touched? A man (not Flanagan) who was paying my rent when I was in my early twenties insisted I see a psychiatrist. I had several sessions with Dr. Pezz, who analyzed that as a child I had not been nurtured by my mother. This was very grave, in Dr. Pezz's mind. It was old news to me. Dr. Pezz ended up being arrested for something, I recall.

Through this night, trucks passed by on the highway, sending their lights through our room, moving crazy shadow shapes up one wall, across the ceiling, down the other wall.

This intense, hungry scenario, it seemed to me finally, was being enacted in my head only. Jed must be asleep. This is a game of intuition, and how trustworthy has my intuition ever been? I know nothing—not what I want, or what is possible, or moral, or true.

I told myself finally, You need to sleep, Holly. You're exhausted with all of this. You have always been exhausted with *all* of this. But I made no decision, I came to no real conclusion. I simply put the tips of my fingers on Jed's smooth forearm and closed my eyes, gave desire and instinct a rest.

It was dark still. I have no idea how many minutes went by. A slight, rhythmical motion awakened me from half-sleep. I remained still, except to open my eyes so it was like the eyes of a child's doll flipping up. He had his right hand, on the side away from me, wrapped around his hard dick and was squeezing. There was a slight trembling of his legs, and his feet were tensed. His left hand, next to me, reached out and touched my neck just by the jaw. I lifted my head. He stroked my throat, then, and his fingernail made a stinging scratch.

We turned toward each other, had our arms round each other's waists. Then we kissed. (I've always been afraid to kiss, a little contemptuous of the act. And mystified by the custom? And shocked by it somehow—it is taboo with me. But Jed and I did kiss, and it required a great leap of faith. I am sad now, remembering that kiss.)

Jed reached down and undid my belt buckle, then the button on my pants, then the zipper. He reached his hand through the fly to feel me, but it was awkward. I clumsily slid my pants down. Jed unbuttoned my shirt and together we worked it over my shoulders and heard a fast, tearing sound.

I pressed Jed back flat on the bed and rolled over on top of him. Our chests were together. I kissed his neck; he rubbed the top of my head, pulling the hair a bit. I slid myself down his small body, holding his ribs like I had a football in each hand. When I had moved far enough down,

I licked the shaft of his dick and it bounced, and I licked it once more as though there actually was something to lick off of it, something to taste and swallow: ice cream?

I took his dick in my mouth, went slowly down, let it touch the back of my throat. From this position I could raise my eyes and see Jed's slender, white naked body, the shoulders tight, his head leaned back so far that only the throat and chin were visible to me. He touched my head, he touched my shoulders, he brought his hands up swiftly and held my ears firmly.

Later, I was standing on the floor. Jed was kneeling before me, with my dick in his mouth—he did not seem to know really what to do, he just held me there, and I felt a sensation of being wrapped in this warm wetness. I moved myself deeper in, then back, in and back. At the same time, Jed was masturbating. His motion got faster, his whole body jerked. I pushed myself into his mouth, gently.

His climax was odd; he seemed to come before he ejaculated. His body tensed and vibrated, he inhaled like he was about to dive in a cold pool and emitted a deep, relieved hum. I felt a splash of hot fluid on my leg, then another. At that instant, Jed bit down on me. I had to grab his shoulders and push him away.

Jed, still kneeling, took hold of my dick with both hands. He pulled it, squeezed, pushed, all rather too hard, too furiously, and I wanted to say, "Gently, Jed, gently," but I could not play his teacher just then. Anyway, there would be plenty of time. I ejaculated onto his chest in one fast, heedless spurt. Jed rubbed the fluid into his chest, spread it over the front of his body.

He rose. We embraced. I'm so much taller than Jed. We maneuvered back over to the bed and folded ourselves under the blanket. We slept deeply; there was no dynamic now of anticipation, intrigue, no sense of a dare. I dreamed of Aunt Joy, recklessly and childishly rocking back and forth on our old wooden porch swing.

This hazy sex, planned and unplanned, occurring sometime between midnight and morning, in the middle of Kansas, in the middle of nowhere, was a vivid puff of smoke. Somehow, indeed, really to touch each other had been one of our contests; but who had made the challenge and who had won was, to me, a mystery. Still is.

We got an early start the next morning. Jed rightly observed that there seemed to be no lake anywhere near the Lakeview Lodge.

Jed

In Las Vegas, I got really sick. So everything that happened is kind of blurry in my memory. It started while we were driving, after we crossed into Nevada from Arizona; my throat felt scratchy and sore and would hurt every time I'd swallow. Also, I kept feeling so, *so* tired, it was really unbelievable. So, I told Holly I didn't feel well. And if I hadn't been so sick, I would have been angry, because he didn't seem to take me seriously, he didn't seem to care, even. He said, well, let's wait until we get to such and such town, and we just kept driving on.

Finally, we pulled into Vegas and got rooms at the Trademark Hotel; Holly registered himself as Dr. Pezz, and me as his son. I think the place was once a pretty fancy hotel, actually, but it was going bankrupt so it was kind of falling apart. Only one of the two elevators ever worked, some bulbs were burned out in those huge, gaudy chandeliers in the lobby, the carpet was worn, etc. And the whole first floor was this noisy, obnoxious casino—slot machines, blackjack tables, ding-ding-dings, and people yelling, and cigar-smoke smell. Which I thought was rather fascinating, but Holly said Vegas gave him a headache and made him nauseous. There was a sign for a show in this kind of cabaret part of the hotel called *Extravaganza!—Nudes on Ice,* and I said we should catch it. I mean, I'd have loved to see something like that, even though I know it's stupid and kind of crass and everything. But Holly said, "Sounds chilly," and kept on walking, tapping his cane, and I followed, of course.

That night, at three or so, I woke up all sweaty and it was like I couldn't catch my breath. Holly threw on pants and a shirt and then he rummaged through his bag and pulled out a thermometer; he's such a hypochondriac, so he has all this stuff, ointments and bandages and pills and stuff. Anyway, my temperature was one-oh-two-point-something, and then Holly was worried. But not just worried—it was like he was irritated, too, like I was interrupting his plans or something. And I even asked him, kind of in an incredulous tone of voice, "Hey, Holly, are you mad at me because I'm sick?"

Which startled him. "Of course not. Of course I'm not angry, Jed."

The next couple of days are hard to remember, they float in a fog: Holly mopping my cheeks and chest with a warm cloth, Holly giving me sips of ginger ale and aspirins. The radio stayed on the whole time, playing talk shows and news, so underneath my fever were these rambling voices, phrases floating through the darkness about homeless people, elections, the Dow Jones average. I remember a hurricane had hit Missouri and the floods buried houses and cars.

This whole sickness thing—it was like one of those old movies where some guy's been in an accident or whatever and his head is all bandaged, he can't see or speak or hear. Then the doctor, the handsome, concerned-looking doctor with gray at his temples, slowly unwraps the gauze bandage and the hospital room—the venetian blinds, the pretty nurse, the medical stuff, etc.—all come gradually into view.

Holly's not exactly the handsome doctor type. I think it was the third morning I started feeling a little bit better. Holly yanked the thermometer from my mouth and looked at it and said, "Well, I'd say the crisis has passed."

He was ready to leave Vegas that afternoon, and I really had to kind of insist we stay on another night. I still just felt too weak. He had taken good care of me, but in a resentful way, sort of. That was so strange to me—I thought Holly, of all people, should understand about sickness. He was sick so much; all his life he'd been weak and physically unfit and everything.

"Jed, you just had a touch of flu."

"I know, well, okay, but I mean I just don't feel strong enough."

"Strong enough for what? To sit in a car?"

"Holly, why can't you let me recuperate a little bit?"

Then he threw up his hands, turned away from me, really angry. He gave in though, he said we could stay one more night. So, I thought Holly was really heartless and everything, mean or whatever. But because of what happened later, I figured out that Holly was just very nervous; he had reasons for wanting to get out, move on.

I was in bed, reading this pretty stupid book about the Civil War—which was Holly's new subject; he said if you can understand the Civil War, you'll understand Americans. The book was putting me to sleep, though. Holly was sitting in a chair, his legs stretched out, his ankles crossed, his hands folded on his chest, his eyes closed. Then there was a knock on the door to our room. Holly's eyes popped open wide, but no other part of him moved. I just looked at Holly, thinking he'd go answer the door, and I started to say something and he shook his head fast, like a visual *shhh*. The knock came again. We stayed still, quiet.

After a minute, Holly closed his eyes again.

Later, I was in a deeper sleep than I'd had during my whole time of sickness, but I heard another knock at the door. Thought I was dreaming or something and then heard it again, a louder, meaner rapping. The room was dark. I saw Holly's shape glide over toward the door and he opened it a crack.

A very deep, gravely voice: "Dr. Pezz?"

Holly whispered, "Yes? What can I do for you? Please speak softly, my son has been quite ill."

"Maybe you'd just step out into the hall here then, so we can talk."

"What is this all about?"

"If you don't mind . . . would you step into the hall?"

Then I could only hear low tones, no words, then I heard nothing. Could have been a minute went by, or an hour. Holly came back into our dark room. He thought I was sleeping and he was real quiet as he packed our things. Then, when he came to bed, he didn't undress or get under the blanket. He stretched out on top and smoked a billion cigarettes. Before it was even daylight, he shook me awake, got me up and dressed. There was no discussion about if I was well or about staying there any longer. We just left.

Then, when we were sputtering down the highway in

the rental car, I asked Holly about the guy who'd come to our room.

"The law."

"What does that mean, what do you mean?" I was kind of hysterically panicked and everything.

"The law. A representative of the law." He asked me to hand him one of his pill bottles.

"Are we in trouble or something?"

"Well, technically, Jed, let's not forget, I *have* kidnapped you. I'd say that's trouble. But it's all been taken care of." He can have this sort of blank, bored attitude about anything, like if you told him a world war had just started, Holly would just shrug, yawn, light a cigarette, or whatever.

"So, wait, that was a policeman or detective or something?"

"Some*body*. Yes. It's over now, though. Forget it."

We drove to the Vegas airport and dropped off our rented car—by this time we'd had about a hundred billion different cars. "I'm tired of driving," Holly said. He bought two airplane tickets using fake names: he called me Billy Jones (after the pet dog he had as a kid) and himself Leslie Flanagan (which I guess he just made up).

So, I was starting to get these little clues—the money, changing cars—that there was a whole lot more to Holly than met the eye. Then Las Vegas. And then Los Angeles. I knew by then that Holly had lots of secrets, this kind of dark part to him, scary but also weirdly exciting.

After we made it through that airport scene with all the people coughing and everything, we got our stuff from the baggage place and practically ran through the airport doors. Right there at the curb, where people are picking up and dropping off, Holly rummaged through one of his

cases, pulled out a bottle of pills, and swallowed a handful
of them. I saw a security guard watching Holly, so I
grabbed his elbow.

Then it was like Holly knew exactly where he was
going. We walked fast through all these parking lots, up
and down rows of cars—I was carrying our stuff, Holly
was walking pretty fast, tapping his cane. And like I said
before, it was really early, about six in the morning, so the
sun was just coming up, everything was tinted a spooky
silvery-orangey color. Then we got to a gold Plymouth,
one of those huge cars, big as a boat, and Holly pulled a
set of keys from his pocket and opened the trunk. He put
all our junk in there and we got in.

"So, whose car is this?" I asked.

"It's our car."

"But I mean how did you know where it was parked
and everything? How long have you had it? Has it just been
sitting here for all this time?"

He asked what difference did it make?

Same thing with our house. Holly drove across all
these freeways, this unbelievable tangle of roads and signs
and exits, cars sliding between each other. By now, the city
had a purplish glow to it. The people on their way to work
had their headlights on, so it looked like little firebugs
darting around. He eased off onto Glendale Boulevard,
twisted through a maze of skinny side streets. And then we
drove up an incline, very steep, practically straight up a
hill, and pulled up to a tiny house. The tiniest house I'd
ever seen, like a kid's doll house or something. There was
a palm tree in front of the door, a squatty little thing with
a fat trunk; it looked like a pineapple. Holly had keys to
this house. We walked in, set down our bags.

"Hey, who lives here, Holly?"

"We live here."

It was basically two rooms and a small kitchen and a small bathroom. The inside was painted kind of a pale yellow color. The furniture looked like it was from the fifties or whatever: a beige studio couch, an oval coffee table, a couple of floor lamps, a wood cabinet, one of those round rugs braided in a spiral. Everything was light, but the place still felt gloomy and small. There was a big picture window in front with venetian blinds covering it.

I had no idea what was going on, I had no clues. I was just following Holly. "How long are we staying here, Holly?"

"Well, let's just say you can go ahead and unpack. There's a closet and plenty of drawer space in the bedroom."

I think I was sort of really mad at Holly because it seemed like he had just been dragging me around all over the country, never telling me our plans. In every big city, Holly would disappear for a whole afternoon, leaving me in a hotel room or at a mall or a movie or something, and then I'd ask him where he'd been, was he seeing friends, or what? Once he said, "Business," but he would never really let me in on anything. He'd just say not to pester him, not to worry.

But I wasn't worried, I was curious. "Where are we going to end up, Holly?" I'd ask and Holly would say, "We'll end up where we end up. Everybody ends up somewhere." He was always saying things like that. And he'd say, "Do you want to go home? Would you rather not come along, Jed?"

Well, I mean, of course, I *did* want to go along. Home? How could I go home? If I went home, I'd miss something, I'd lose Holly. I knew what life at home was; but life with

Holly was like a puzzle, and I wanted to know how it all fit. I wanted to learn more from Holly. I never once thought of turning back.

So, finally, I got the picture: where we were going to end up was Los Angeles, California. I thought, Who wants to end up *here?*

Holly said he was exhausted, that we'd talk in the morning, that he was going to bed. He did, and I joined him. I remember that first night we both were lying on our backs, far apart, on opposite edges of the bed. Some dog was barking really meanly, wouldn't stop. I was kind of staring at the ceiling in the dark, thinking. Feeling like I loved Holly but I didn't really know him. That he was my family now, but he was a stranger. I was taking deep breaths and telling myself not to cry. You know how you can feel all alone even when you're with someone you know loves you? Like some kind of little alien child, lost on earth.

And the next morning Holly had prepared coffee and juice and toast. He was reading the paper and when I came shuffling in with a blanket wrapped around me, he looked up, very calmly, blinked in that slow way he had and said, "We'll probably need guns in this city, Jed." Which I thought was very funny.

Rather quickly actually, I started to like L.A. For those first few days, Holly and I just hung around our new little house. I felt good finally to be stopped in one place, to get settled. Our garage was crammed with boxes and trunks—Holly's stuff from over the years—and we went through it all. We put pictures up on the walls, we put books on shelves.

On one side our neighbor was an old man; we only saw him when he walked his poodle dogs. On the other side the house was all boarded up with a FOR RENT sign on the door. Our house had a back porch, too, made of cracked concrete, and there was a steep slope of a hill right beneath it, all wild and green, with lemon and plum trees. You could see a freeway, rooftops. You could see mountains far away. From the back door, when the sky was clear—which it never *really* was—you could see a little stripe of white that was that famous HOLLYWOOD sign.

In the afternoons, I took off my clothes and laid on a blanket out on the porch. The air always smelled like gasoline and flowers. It was very quiet up on this hill, actually, except for the sirens.

We drove around a lot, because you have to drive in L.A. The streets are wide and lined with strips of stores and car lots. Every part of the city looks like every other part, just strips of stores and car lots. I complained to Holly about this, I said I thought everything was really ugly. He said, "Just wait." And one evening, right at sunset, we got in the car and drove down Hollywood Boulevard, past all the tacky auto repair shops and fast food restaurants and the revolving signs advertising doctors and doughnuts and real estate. Holly pulled over to a parking spot and pointed to a square whitewashed building with giant blue plastic letters—CAR WASH—on the roof. Now the sun was almost down and this building was half in shadow.

"That's what you call 'bathing' light," Holly told me. "It's only in the desert and, you know, Los Angeles is really just a desert. Look at that." He pointed to the car wash place. It was pretty spectacular, actually—golden, almost glowing where the sun hit, and like charcoal in the shadow, and the words in blue were bright against the hazy, cloudless, blue sky.

Holly's idea, the reason he took me to see the building

at sunset, was that everybody might think something is stupid and ugly, but that's only because they don't really know how to look at it. "It isn't what is there, Jed. It's your way of seeing. Goethe said, 'Every form correctly seen is beautiful.' "

"It is beautiful," I said, and we sat and looked at the car wash place for a while longer, watched the shadow and light move. "It's like a picture."

That was the day I got my camera. A Leica Holly had in a box in the garage. He had a Polaroid, too, and another camera, a pretty expensive old-fashioned one; but that Leica is what I fell in love with. Different lenses and fairly complicated settings and everything, and no instructions, so I had to figure everything out myself. I started shooting two or three rolls of film every afternoon and I'd make Holly drive me down to the photo place, then make him take me back to get the pictures.

At first, mostly everything I shot was out of focus. So Holly got me some books on photography. We talked about composition, we talked about why I might want to shoot some subjects in black-and-white but others in color and how to make those decisions. Holly told me that the film is coated with silver and memory is silver too. "You simultaneously must create and observe your own aesthetic," Holly said. "Watch your own impulses with the camera, and then cultivate, manipulate."

With my camera . . . I was off. Free, kind of, or grown-up or something. Definitely, I was different. The camera became my eye. I was in love, really, in love with pictures, with my Leica, with the rolls of film and the cleaning stuff. But it was mostly the shooting, the experience. It was like taking drugs or something. I spent one day down at the Tropical Bakery, a little dive coffee shop on

Sunset—I must have used five rolls of film. Pictures of the pastry cases, the espresso machines, the signs and stools and counter. And every single person in that place—old Cuban guys playing dominoes, kids, fags and hippies, and women with briefcases.

I tried to explain to Holly what was happening to me. I remember especially one night lying on the bed side by side, but in opposite directions, so my feet were next to his face, his feet next to mine. "It's almost like I've been afraid to look at the world because it might be too beautiful or too ugly. But then you gave me my camera and everything is beautiful *and* ugly. I mean, it doesn't matter, or something. I can . . . filter everything I see, make something out of it."

"You're an artist, Jed. That's what you're describing."

"Well, whatever, I don't know. I just know I'm really happy, Holly."

He put his fingers on my toes, pulled my toes against his cheek. And then he didn't say anything for a while. And then, without thinking at all, without knowing what I was saying or why, I suddenly sat up and asked, "Don't you want me to be happy, Holly?"

"I do, Jed. I do," he answered—so sad, so far away. He wrapped his arms around my bare legs, turned his face into the pillow. I had the most bizarre urge to snap a picture of him then; but I didn't do it.

Holly

Jed did not think of us as sinister, which is what made him so remarkable. He was beyond his years in wisdom and intelligence—but many boys are. What saved Jed, and astounded me, was his extraordinary self-possession. I saw it in the photographs he took, and it scared me. How preposterous that I was stuttering out my theories and quotes and definitions, desperate to teach him. I was simply afraid that Jed was maturing, getting smarter and healthier and stronger, and that he would inevitably go away. Like what poor Rev. Dodgson must have felt with his tough little Alice—a terrible unrequitedness, a sorrowful certainty that he is only another game to be outgrown. (And, of course, look how I treated Flanagan.)

I was automatically irritated by Jed's photographs—looking at them, discussing them, thinking about them. Jed knew I was resentful at his enterprise, his movement toward some interest that did not involve me. Photographs as objects are loathsome and terrifying to me. A photograph captures a moment, epitomizes a person's vision. It will stimulate memory and desire; conjure up, like magic, all the pettiness and failure and frenzy. A series of photographs is a chronicle of innocence slipping away. If you've had a good life, you are comforted and pleased with pictures. If you've had a bad life, you are morbidly intrigued. If you've had my kind of life, though, you'll stare at pictures and only feel lost.

We came across a photograph when Jed and I were sorting through my boxes in the garage. The frame was cheap, wooden, and the glass had been broken and discarded long ago. The picture was printed on thick card stock, black-and-white with a sepia tone, yellow-gold with age at the edges. It showed a woman leaning over a wicker basket in which a smiling baby lay, its bald head resting on a satiny pillow. The baby's tiny arms were outstretched, its fingers urging the mother forward. The mother wore a print dress, her hair set in a common style of the period: 1950 or so. She is reaching for her child and smiling, but the expression and posture are so contrived, posed for the camera. In fact, while the baby's smile is genuine, the mother's is utterly false. The baby trusts, the mother does not.

When Jed discovered this terrible thing, he said, "Hey, is this your mother? Is this you?"

Jed

Holly gave me a test. He said, "There is one thing everyone needs so badly that they will do absolutely anything they have to in order to get it. It's something that causes war, causes happiness, makes the laws. It is the basis of all society and human life. What is this one thing?"

"Love?"

"Of course not."

"Sex?"

"No."

"Children?"

"Children? No."

"Religion?"

"Oh, you're really reaching now, Jed."

I guessed a lot more things, but, actually, I had no idea what he was talking about. The answer, it turned out, was money.

We were sitting in our living room, drinking iced tea, listening to this weird Delibes record—ladies singing, but they sounded like they were being strangled. It was very hot that evening, so we kept the door open. Holly kind of shrugged his shoulders and said, "Everyone needs money, Jed."

That was how I started going to work. He was very plain with me, he said right out that he knew I would do quite well if I went with men for cash. He said the money would support us comfortably and there would be enough to put aside for me when I was older. He said he hoped I didn't object to having sex with strangers; he would understand if I didn't want to do it, but he asked me to give it serious thought. "If I could do it, I would, Jed. I did, in fact. But I don't have those talents anymore, I don't have that appeal. One must surrender gracefully. So, I will do what I'm good at, and you'll do what you're good at."

Holly put ads in all the L.A. gay newspapers and magazines. There is this way you can word the ad that makes it sound legitimate, like you're not really a prostitute—you call yourself a model or something—but the people who read the ads know what to look for. I was fourteen when this whole thing started—Holly and I had celebrated my birthday on the road. So the words in the ad were like *Boy Bliss* or *Chicken Delight* or something stupid like that. Holly handled everything. He talked to the men on the phone, he set the price, he made the appointments. This operation was rather complicated because prostitution is illegal, but, as Holly told me, boy prostitution is *really* illegal.

He would drive me to a hotel or apartment house or whatever and wait outside in our gold Plymouth, reading and smoking cigarettes. He was fairly strict about things.

He found out exactly what these men were interested in before we got there. He told me what to say, how to act, that I should get the money up front. He told me I should agree to do anything they asked me to, but the weirder it got, the more money I should demand. He said most of these guys were completely harmless, they were bored or lonely, they had some fantasy in their minds and were willing to pay to act it out. But Holly did give me some safety precautions. Don't let the guy lock the door with a key. Don't let my clothes out of my sight. Don't drink or smoke anything with the guy. He made a big point that I never had to kiss anyone. And if I ever felt any real sense of danger, or anything made me think the guy was a nut, I should follow my own instincts. "You have impeccable instincts, Jed. Be polite, give back the money, and walk out."

It was impossible to figure out if Holly had a particular opinion or judgment about any of this. We needed money, this was a way to get it. He did say he didn't think this line of work was right for every boy, but he thought I could take it. It wasn't that he thought it was any kind of wonderful thing for me to be doing; but he didn't think it was causing me any harm either. He treated the whole thing like a job, like he was driving me to work at a supermarket or coffee shop or whatever.

Now, for me, all of this was a really terrific adventure—at first anyway. The men were old guys, mostly, with pot bellies, maybe losing their hair, and a lot of them—especially the ones I met in hotel rooms—had really dry lips and goofy looks on their faces like they were starving or something. These men all had a thing about having sex with little boys. So, I walked in, fourteen years old, but I looked even younger I guess. I was like an actor, playing the part of a cute little boy, a pretty boy who only wanted some man to suck him off. It's all a pretense. That's what Holly told me.

So, the sex with these men didn't mean much to me. I called them customers. Holly called them patients. Anyway, with the customers I would close my eyes and just let myself drift with the physical sensation. But I did feel a powerful kind of rush, when I'd leave the man, when the door closed behind me. Like I had won a prize or gotten away with stealing. It was weirdly satisfying.

I could never quite explain this feeling to Holly. Maybe he didn't care what it was like for me; or maybe he already knew.

Holly

Well, finally, mine is the simplest kind of story—a little fable. Mama was always telling me to go outside and play. I did not like play. I felt confused and pressured at the thought of play.

"Mama, I don't feel too good."

"No? Well, neither do I, Hollis."

I would make drawings sometimes. I wish I could look at them today, to analyze my beginnings, to see if I can observe, in the clumsy, aimless crayon lines, the loss of myself.

I liked to read, but not children's books—I was more interested in the mystery and romance novels Aunt Joy had half-finished and left strewn about the house.

One wet, dark September morning—the first day of fourth grade—I stocd miserably on the county road waiting for the school bus, wearing my yellow slicker, holding my book bag. Terrified. Oh, of everything. The approach of the bus, the driver. The other children, especially. Then, fearful of the teachers, the classroom, the corridors, lunchtime, and playtime. The games and stories and even the lessons of school were profoundly threatening to me; I knew I was alone there, yet I was pulled into a thousand interactions, into a context of camaraderie and normal life.

I was convinced, heart and soul, that these journeys to school, into the outside world, were dangerous. I would be hit or insulted. I would be deprived and hurt and misunderstood. It was clear to me that all these children knew some crucial thing about life that I did not know.

It was not at all my choice to extend my experience beyond what I knew—our house, Mama and Aunt Joy, Asylum Street's spooky and protecting shade.

Every September I began this treacherous, relentless struggle. In fourth grade, though, I found God. I prayed for God to keep me safe on the long ride to the schoolhouse. I prayed to survive the morning. I prayed to survive the afternoon. I prayed to be inconspicuous. I prayed to be delivered to my home.

At night, in my bed, I prayed, "Don't make me go back tomorrow. Make something happen where I don't have to go back." I thought, but would not say aloud to God: Well, I don't *think* I *really* want to die, but if it's the only way not to have to go back to school, let me die in my sleep tonight.

What a tragic, haunting mixture of sadness and relief I would feel when I awoke, quite alive, the next day.

All the children but me waited for snow. I was frightened of snow. Mean boys might throw snowballs at my neck. A kid might trip me on the ice, and then everyone would see me cry.

Of course, one day the snow did come. We all wore
hats and mittens and scarves. When I returned from
school, heartsick, fundamentally separate from the cheer
and sport of the new winter, and stepped into our kitchen,
Aunt Joy was at the table. The radio was not on. She
rushed to me.

"I'm going to make us some hot chocolate," she said,
kneeling before me, looking me directly in the eye. "I
don't want you to worry, Holly." She unwrapped my
layers of winter wear, guided me to the wooden chair at
the table. "And we'll . . . we can light a fire. Won't that
be nice?" She went quickly to the stove, poured milk into
a saucepan.

"Where's Mama? Is she back from Asylum Street?"

Aunt Joy started to cry. She could not help herself.

A bird landed on our windowsill and danced on one
foot. "Can we have a little birdhouse for that bird, Aunt
Joy?"

Aunt Joy took the dish towel and buried her face in it
with a fast, furious motion. Her red hair fell across her
forehead. In a moment, she looked at me and her face was
as red as her hair.

Now she knelt before me again, put a hand on each of
my knees. She told me Mama had got very sick. The doctor
had had to come, and then they took Mama away. They did
not know when she would be back home.

I said, "How come she's sick? Did she have a temperature?"

"Yes, she did, she did have a temperature."

"Did her head ache like it always does?"

"Yes, Holly. Her head was hurting very badly."

"Was she screaming?"

Aunt Joy looked past me, distracted. Maybe she watched that bird. "She was screaming, Holly. She was screaming and I was scared she would just never stop."

Through our journey, our dusty, fast, dangerous trek across America, there was much I kept from Jed. That he was only a boy—I kept that from Jed.

And I kept from him the ominous reality of our situation: that we were in flight, that by any conventional standard, he was my victim and I his captor. I felt lost, though pleasantly so, in some dreamy, incomprehensible displacement, where I had no childhood: Jed's youth was mine. I existed in relation to Jed, as his protector, as the adult. Jed was such a perfect boy, not layered with shame and apprehension and weakness.

We were in Phoenix for Jed's fourteenth birthday. Browsing through a pawn shop, I came upon a Boy Scout uniform, with accompanying scarf and badges. I bought the uniform for Jed. When we were back at Stacey's Welcome Home Inn, located directly under a freeway overpass, Jed consented to dress up in this khaki and olive green ensemble. He did not know the credo or even how to salute. I told him I had a fantasy of being seduced by a Boy Scout, and he rolled his eyes but enacted the role generously, playfully, laughing. He pushed me onto the floor, in a corner, and fucked me fast. I shut my eyes and tried to envision the Boy Scouts I had seen as a child—sexy, somewhat sinister, terribly self-important youths—conjured up a delicious image of being raped by a gang of them. Rape has not meant much to me for some years, as it happens; indeed, I had overestimated the thrill of a Boy Scout. So that fantasy faded, leaving the splendid truth, what was actual—that earnest, delightful Jed, thriftier and braver than anyone, that this little boy was digging his fingers into my bony hips and pushing his slender dick inside me with such force, with no contrivance. It was a sincere fuck; and that's such a rare thing.

Later, he said, "You know, that uniform was really for *you*. Don't I get a present that's for *me*?" Very smart, disarming and sweet and humorous. Jed was a perfect boy. I remember thinking, after he'd fallen to sleep, that I could well understand why some kidnappers lock their stolen children away in basement rooms, attics, even in cages: not as punishment, not from a cruel impulse, but simply to keep them, as treasure. I should have put Jed in a box; today I would know where he is.

Another thing I kept from Jed, of course, was that two or three days after we fled Lila's house, I had telephoned her. *"Mr.* Flood," she cooed menacingly. "I wondered when you'd call."

"You got my note, Mrs. Levine?" I had left a brief explanation of Jed's and my mutual decision for her, stuck to the refrigerator door with a magnet.

"Of course I got your note. I called the police immediately and told them you were a deranged kidnapper and they're hunting you down this very minute. Where the hell is Jed? Where's my boy?"

I was thinking, Her boy? He's *my* boy. But, of course, he's nobody's boy. A boy cannot belong to someone, cannot be possessed by someone. No one owns Jed.

"Jed is fine," I said. "The fact is, you know, Jed prefers to be with me. The moment he wishes to go home, back to you, he certainly will. He is learning a great deal. He is healthy."

"Listen, you son of a bitch——"

"We are traveling, and our route is unplanned. This entire kidnapping was quite spontaneous, Mrs. Levine."

There was a second of silence. "I guess it's too much to hope for that you're not some kind of fag pervert." I might mention that Mrs. Levine was in no way distraught, she did not even seem worried. She was simply furious.

"I can tell you I love Jed."

"Yes. That's what I thought." I could hear her suck on her cigarette and blow out the smoke.

"Jed loves me, too, Mrs. Levine."

"Well, you listen to me, you fucking lunatic. The police are going to find you. They're going to get you. And *fry* you. Do you hear me?"

"I better go. I will call again some day. I'll suggest that Jed write you, but, of course, I can't promise he'll choose to."

"You're sick. You truly are sick," she was bellowing, and I wanted to ask what she meant by that, what she could *possibly* mean by that, but I had to hang up.

I dared not phone Jed's mother again, fearing the police would trace the calls. Throughout our travels, here and there I would purchase a postcard from a hotel or gift shop, scribble a quick message, such as, "All's well here, hope you're fine, Love Hollis Flood and Jed,"—designed to, at once, irritate and reassure. After all, she *was* the boy's mother. But, I never mailed them—too risky, I did not want her to know our route. Jed never did know of my actual communication.

Some places the police cars are black and white, some are blue and white, there are even some painted lime green and white. Depends on the county. I never sped, always followed all traffic regulations. When I saw the police, I would signal and glide whatever rental car we happened to have onto a side street, into a driveway, pretend to look at a map, and hold my breath.

We'd check into motels, places along the highway, after dark. I'd leave Jed in the car and when I'd go into the office to register I would leave my cane behind, wear a hat and reading glasses, in case there was a description of me floating around. I'd say, "My little boy's asleep in the car." The person at the desk, usually an older woman at such places, would smile—the phrase "my little boy" is somehow comforting and heartwarming for people. "Oh, yes," I'd say, shrugging, "he's getting so big, I can't even carry him into the room anymore." Another smile. Maybe some talk about her son: in college or killed in a war or married. And I am, for a moment, fraudulently a part of that normal world in which people do legitimately own their children. Then, once in our room, inevitably there would be a faraway sound of a siren and flashing red and blue lights rushing down the empty, lonely highway; standing at the window I would grip the edge of the curtain, breathless, knowing this might be for me. Caught. I was never at ease. Eventually, some kindly motel clerk lady will look at my face with a special scrutiny, will strain to see past me to the boy in the car, will make the connection of recognition and see in her own future the rewards of good, righteous citizenship. We *will* get caught, I was always thinking.

Las Vegas was it. The Trademark Hotel. Because Jed had been running a fever, we'd had to stay on longer than I thought was safe. Jed slept. His black hair was wet and plastered to his temples. His cheeks were pink. I was not much worried about his health, really—clearly he'd just caught a bug and was exhausted.

(I have vivid recollections of my own childhood fevers and Aunt Joy's ministrations: she would pass a soft, warm, damp cloth over my chest and neck and forehead and apply a menthol gel to my throat. With her husky whisper, soft so she would not disturb Mama, Aunt Joy would read aloud to me: " 'Scarlett was done with passion and marriage. She was done with marriage but not with love, for her love for Ashley was something different, having nothing to do with passion or marriage, something sacred and breath-takingly beautiful, an emotion that grew stealthily through the long days of her enforced silence, feeding on oft-thumbed memories and hopes.' "

"Are you like Scarlett, Aunt Joy?"

"Oh, no, oh, Holly, no, don't be silly," but I saw how she loved that idea, that she fantasized her own fiery independence and beauty and ambition.)

Late night. Someone knocked on the door. I ignored it of course, and then the knock came again, insistent. I grabbed a roll of cash. The way someone else might reach for a gun for protection, I go for cash. I opened the door a crack.

"Dr. Pezz?" I had registered under that name.

I whispered, "Yes? What can I do for you? Please speak softly, my son has been quite ill."

Standing before me, in the cruel white light of the corridor was a short, overweight man in a suit and vest, wearing a hat, smoking a cigar. His shoes were brown. Without doubt, a cop. "Maybe you'd just step out into the hall here then, so we can talk."

"What is this all about?"

"If you don't mind . . . would you step into the hall?"

I did. He flipped a weathered brown billfold in front

of me, showing me his badge. "Detective Millett. Is your name Hollis Flood?" Well, he knew it was.

"No. No, it's Arnold Pezz. *Dr.* Arnold Pezz." This I declared righteously, seeming offended at the intrusion.

"I'll need to see some ID then," said the round little man, shifting the cigar across his teeth to the other side of his disbelieving, hostile face.

I looked at the closed door to our room, then back at Millett. "Would you mind just stepping over here, I really don't want to wake my son, he's been ill," and I began to walk toward the door to the staircase.

There will be other cops, I was thinking. There will be a couple of cops in uniform nearby. I pushed the heavy EXIT door and held it open with my foot at the same time I brought forth my wallet. Millett waddled swiftly after me, not intending for one second to risk this kidnapper's escape.

We were in the harshly lit stairwell now, all cinderblock with iron railings, painted a cream color. He looked over my cards, all of which, of course, were for a Dr. Arnold Pezz, with my photo and description. I always keep plenty of ID. He stuck a pinky finger in his ear, deep, and wiggled it around. He handed the wallet back to me. "That's bullshit, Flood. Is the kid in the room?"

Now I was profoundly indignant. "Excuse me, Detective, to what precinct of the police department are you assigned?"

"Huh? Precinct? Listen, you: I'm the house detective. My precinct is this goddamn hotel." Our voices echoed in the stairwell, so we were whispering. "There's flyers out everywhere about a guy named Hollis Flood who kidnapped a kid named Something-or-Other. And you're him, and that's the kid," he declared, pointing over his shoulder with his thumb, with the self-importance of an umpire calling an out.

Oh, a house detective; well, he's nobody, then. But I feigned confusion and slight panic and stuttered, "Me? Detective, I mean, I can assure you, whoever you're looking for, I really hope they find the man, it all sounds just awful, but me? I can assure you—"

"Yeah, you can assure me. Sure." His face was bloated, criss-crossed with red veins and scars of old blemishes.

He was not going to believe me. A long moment passed, silent but for a buzzing ice machine on the landing beneath us. Without hesitation, but with no particular pith either—rather as a simple gesture made toward a good friend—I pulled the roll of bills from my shirt pocket, stretched out my arm, held the money in my fist.

He lifted his chin as a question.

"That's a thousand dollars," came my whisper-echo.

"Oh, a thousand dollars, huh? That's pretty funny, Flood." He looked at the floor, scraped the toe of one of his horrid, cracked brown shoes against a stair.

"My son and I will be leaving before morning," I said.

Minutes went by with neither of us moving; it was the most hideous kind of contest, but I knew I would win. Finally, without looking at me, he reached over and took the roll of bills from my hand, thrust it in his trousers pocket. He bit down hard on the foul cigar; he adjusted his hat.

"Thank you, Detective," I said.

Still looking down, the tubby creep said, "Well. Well. I really shouldn't do this."

No, I was thinking, No, you shouldn't, so why do you,

you hypocritical shit? No, none of us should be doing half of what we do.

Then we were stonewalled. I did not know how to pass him, to get back into the hotel corridor, when to leave, what would signal that this interaction was finished; he was at as much of a loss. Finally, he stepped to the side. He abruptly turned his back to me, so he was now facing the ascending set of stairs. I put my hand on the door handle, ready to go, relieved and satisfied for a second; and then I had to glance back. I looked at his broad back, grotesquely stretching the cheap suit. His neck was bright red, a thick fold rolling over his stiff shirt collar. This was a guilty, petty little man. A man who probably had some kids and a wife, paid a hooker now and then, liked his cigar, cried when Kennedy was shot, thought he'd go to heaven.

(I had been in exactly this emotional spot many times throughout my life. So, it was not a *déja vu,* which is some sort of mysterious psychic trick, an illusion; this was truly a familiar moment, representing so many repeated sad mistakes. It is a mistake, I suppose, to take advantage of people's bad natures, their self-serving tendencies, as well as to exhibit my own. And we can go on and on and on, doing the wrong thing, using these small gestures, and we can count on others to do the wrong thing. How untrue are the messages of literature and cinema, which give us the good guy and bad guy.

I was thinking, I must talk to Jed about all of this, about literature and cinema, good guys and bad guys. "The hardest and most important lesson you will learn, Jed," I planned to say, "is that people are capable of absolutely anything."

In a quick dream, like a scratchy old black-and-white
movie, I saw myself lift my hands, flat, with the fingers
spread, and move slowly toward the dull brown fabric
across that thick back. The hands pressed—gently, carelessly, almost as though they were pushing through a soft
wave. My hands were beautiful, slender with pale blue
veins.

The frame widens, the angle changes. It is not a gentle
push. Millett falls hard and suddenly against the stone steps
and crashes onto his knees. He is taken so by surprise that
he does not even cry out but begins to lift himself up. I
push him down again. A close shot of my face, now: fierce
brow, tight mouth, burning, raging, stunning eyes. I put
both of my hands on the back of his head, behind the ears
and under the hat brim, and throw him down like I am
smashing a watermelon on a curb. Millett's hat slides off
his head. I pick up his head by the ears and pound it again
on the corner of a stair, which is covered now with running
veins of dark red blood. And again, and this time blood
spurts from his head or eyes or mouth, splaying a design
on the wall. Again, again, again.

Close shot of my graceful, perfectly shaped hands as
they pull the roll of money from the detective's pocket.)

As I exited the stairwell, Millett's gurgling, sharp
cough destroyed my vicious daydream. He was quite alive.
We were both cowards, both aiming to protect ourselves
and both somewhat richer for the exchange. I moved
soundlessly back to our room. I packed our things that
night. I woke Jed just as my watch hit 4:00 A.M. We were
silent in the elevator and walked briskly through the lobby,
crowded even then with people glued by compulsive, silly
hope to their lucky slot machines—people's superstitions

can be so extraordinary. Jed followed me sleepily, without question.

We settled into the car and I drove slowly through the bright, flashing reds and greens of the strip, past neon signs of cowboys and tits and stars, out of that town, away. What a perverse and cloudy exhilaration there was to our flight and the crime I'd done; and I carried an even heartier, more breathless feeling about the crime I'd only dreamed.

(Aunt Joy used to steal makeup from the Woolworth's in town and she'd tell me how she felt as she was leaving the store: with cheap lipsticks and perfume samples in her purse, she would walk slowly, steadily toward the front door and feel the eyes of customers and clerks, fearfully and excitedly imagine the fingers of a guard suddenly around her elbow, imagine the sound of someone barking, "Young lady, young lady." But Aunt Joy kept walking down the aisles, pushing all odds, defying the possibilities, and she'd emerge finally onto the sunny, crowded, safe street. Her small crime delighted her. She always got away with it. Another thing I adored about Aunt Joy.)

There were few people waiting at our gate at that hour. I sat smoking, sipping coffee from a styrofoam cup. Jed stood before the giant window, his back to me as he leant against a pillar and looked out onto the empty, wet runway. I desired Jed very desperately, then. His tenderness, sincerity. His tiny, white ankles, his slim dick. His ignorance. A kiss from Jed.

And I was suddenly panicked; I keenly felt, as I never really had, the gravity of my situation, of my responsibilities toward Jed. I felt inadequate. Wishing to make a safe world for Jed, the best I could do was pay off a puny cop and then escape into an echoing stairwell and a dream of murder. Running, running, all my life I'd seen some twist of bravery in my defections. Now, dragging this boy with me, taking him from the imperfection I perceived in his home, to what? To my own imperfection. And was this life for him or for me? For him or for me?

Jed

So, the spookiest, craziest trick or customer or whatever you call them was this guy named Timothy. And, what's especially rather weird, is that I believe Holly really knew what he was sending me into. When he dropped me off that evening at the apartment building in the Los Feliz section, Holly grabbed my elbow, looked me in the eye.

"What, Holly? What's the problem? I'm running late, you know."

"Just remember; don't be afraid. There's nothing to be afraid of. Think of all this as research."

I got out of the car, walked through a gate and across a little stone courtyard with red lights shining from under bushes. I went to Number 9 and knocked and looked out at the street, at Holly waiting in the car, flaring a match to light his cigarette.

Timothy ushered me in like I was the best friend he hadn't seen in a billion years. Then he kind of scurried around, closing the blinds, locking the door. He was a mousy man; small, hunched, balding even though he was probably not even thirty years old, not even Holly's age. He wore a white shirt, with a bunch of pens and a glasses case in the pocket, and black pants. No shoes. He took my hand in both of his and pressed, smiled at me. "You're Jed. Lovely to meet you, Jed. I am Timothy." When he let go of my hand, he turned away; there was a roll of twenty dollar bills in my hand and I stuck it in my pocket.

He had old-fashioned big band music on the radio, soft, not the real raucous kind. "Juice?" His voice was squeaky, high, nervous.

"Yes, sure, okay, I'd take some juice." Even though I'm not supposed to drink anything these guys offer.

"Oh, lovely, yes, that's fine then," he went on as he opened this tiny refrigerator and brought out a bottle of cranberry juice. He had plastic cups and poured for each of us.

Now, this room of Timothy's was practically empty. There was a single bed—just a thin matress on a plain metal frame—very tidily made up, like a bed at Boy Scout camp or something. Next to the bed was a nightstand with a little lamp, the radio, an ashtray. There was a dresser against another wall and the little refrigerator. No chairs or anything, no desk or shelves. The carpet was drab, dark green.

Then, hanging on the white wall, above his bed, was this enormous crucifix—maybe three feet tall. It had a carved figure of Christ, draped, with the crown of thorns, with the long hair and beard. The figure was painted cream color for the skin, brown for the cloth and hair, and bright red for blood at his side and hands and temples.

I walked toward this incredible thing, trying to look closer. "Jesus," I said.

"Do you like him?" I heard from behind me, and turned around to see Timothy wringing his fingers, licking his lips.

"Yeah, well, sure."

"I made him."

"No kidding?"

"That's right. I sculpted him myself. Made entirely of wood."

"You must be pretty religious and everything."

Timothy said, "I'm a Lutheran." Then he started laughing, almost like when people are fake laughing in a play or in a movie, and then all of a sudden he was crying. I just stood there. I get really nervous when people are crying. I want to go help them and everything, but it's like I get paralyzed. And then, just as suddenly as he had laughed and cried, he stopped. He sat on the edge of the bed.

"Can you come beside me?" he asked, in a whisper.

I moved over to him and sat. He put his hand over my hand. "You're not any kind of wild boy. I know that." When he spoke, he looked at the floor, not at me. So, I was watching the side of his face: the bony jaw, crinkles around his eyes. "You're good, Jed. I want some of your goodness to rub off onto me. Do you understand?"

"Yes. Yes, I think I understand. But maybe I'm not all that good."

"No. You're good."

"Well, I mean, are you so bad?"

He moved his hand and put it over my crotch, very

gently, just held it there. He bit his lip. He nodded his head. A tear came down his cheek.

"Hey, hey, Timothy."

And then he was biting his lip harder, and a little blood squirted out. Which really shocked me. I mean, my instinct was to get out of there, my intuition or whatever told me this was a rather sick person. But I didn't know what to do or say.

Timothy got up and from under the bed brought out these little votive candles in glass jars, ten or twelve of them. He placed them around the room and lit them, turned off the ceiling light.

He climbed on the bed and grasped the giant crucifix, held it by Christ's arms, and kind of unhooked the whole thing from the wall. It seemed heavy. I asked if he wanted me to help him, but he did not answer. He laid the crucifix down on the bed.

Then he stretched out beside this Jesus on the cross, put his arm over the painted wooden ribs and chest, kind of pushed his little mouse face into Jesus' wooden neck. And he didn't say anything more, he didn't move. I just stood beside the bed watching him, watching orange candle flickers. A siren screamed outside.

I was very frightened then. Is he asleep? Maybe he's dead or something or just crazy or something. After five minutes like this, I turned away. I walked to the bathroom door, I was going to go in the bathroom, I couldn't think what else to do.

But Timothy said, "I'm excited, Jed."

I turned around.

"I'm excited now, Jed. Come over here."

I went to him, stood above him, looking down.

"Kneel by the bed," Timothy told me, very breathless and whispery. I did kneel. "Okay, okay, okay," Timothy went on, "okay, now pray for me, Jed."

"What? I don't know—what do you mean?"

"Please. Pray for me, Jed."

Mostly, I was scared. I didn't know what was coming next. I thought this man might be some insane religious nut murderer or something. But I folded my hands, like little kids do when they're saying their prayers at night.

"God . . ."

"Whisper, Jed, whisper your prayers." He held tighter to his Jesus, pressed his body up against the figure, and it seemed like he was holding his breath.

I whispered, "God, please take care of Timothy." I didn't have even the littlest idea what he wanted from me, but I just kept praying. "Make Timothy good. Make Timothy feel like he's a good person, and not feel so . . . ashamed and bad and everything."

"Yes," said Timothy. "Yes." He was kind of sliding his hips around now against the leg of Jesus.

"God, show Timothy a sign that he's a good person, so he won't feel guilty and bad and lonely. Give Timothy happiness and joy and love."

"Yes," Timothy was shouting-whispering, his eyes shut tight, his whole body trembling, clutching this wooden body next to him. "Yes, pray that I'll know God."

"And let Timothy know you, God."

"That I won't suffer here or after my death."

"Don't make Timothy suffer, God, not here or after death."

"And pray for yourself, Jed. Pray for yourself, Jed, please, pray for yourself."

Real quick, I said, "Take care of me, too, God. Help me have a good life."

"Oh, oh, lovely, oh, say that again, Jed," Timothy ordered me, and I did, and again. "Okay, okay. Fine, okay," Timothy said, breathing hard now. He reached out and put a hand on my head, gently pushed my head down so it rested on my arms.

We stayed this way for what seemed like a long time. Everything was quiet. I realized Timothy had fallen asleep. A couple of the candles had burned out.

I handed Holly the roll of bills when I got back to the car; there were five twenties. Usually Holly asked me some question—how did it go, was I all right, was I hungry?—but this night, he just started the car, we eased off down the smooth, empty street, like it was in a dream.

I was thinking how sad it is that people feel so guilty about things. And then they end up, I guess, with these really bizarre perversions to help them deal with how guilty they feel. I thought Timothy was a very pitiful person. Because he hated himself and he was trapped with himself, he couldn't change, he just acted out the same strange scene.

So then I looked over at Holly. "Holly? When you were hustling and everything when you were a kid, did you ever feel sorry for some of these men?"

"No."

"You never felt that they were kind of sad or something?"

"No. Never."

Just then we pulled into our little drive, Holly shut off the car. I said, "Well, I don't want to go back to that guy, to that Timothy guy."

"That's fine, Jed. You don't have to."

"I think he's sick."

"Really? Sick?" And Holly was out of the car, was walking calmly into our house.

Holly

One night I sat in the driver's seat, remembering inaccurately lines from Eliot. "Wavering between the profit and the loss/In this brief transit where the dreams cross" blah blah blah. "This is the time of tension between dying and birth" blah blah blah. "Suffer me not to be separated." And wondering if I still had power over Jed enough to sit him down with Eliot, marking up the books, praising or denouncing, intriguing him, my boy. Or was that all gone?

Dead street, very late. I smoked and smoked, while Jed was inside, playing who-knew-what kind of silly, sick prayer games? Timothy had been an ordained Lutheran minister once but was kicked out for fondling boys from the parish. Timothy's deeply suicidal, I think.

Smoking and remembering Dr. Pezz. I told this professional that I was not interested in psychology.

"What, then?"

"Phenomena, I suppose."

"Go on."

"I am interested in Aunt Joy. I want to talk about Aunt Joy," said I. "Not my mother, but my aunt, Joy."

"Well that seems like a fine place to start."

But then I was irritated. "I do not have a pathology, Doctor, for you to evaluate. That's misguided. My problem, if I have a problem, is a moral one."

"Go on."

"I'm amoral. I cannot make moral decisions."

"And what is your sense of that?"

"I don't have a *sense* of it. I am a victim of life, can't you see that? You want to develop practical solutions, you want to talk about coping with situations. All of that is irrelevant, it doesn't apply. My problem is fundamental, Dr. Pezz. It's deep."

"You're quite agitated right now, Hollis. What is it you think you need?"

"A heart transplant. Find me someone else's heart."

"I guess you think you're being amusing."

Then I just told that doctor I thought he was an idiot, and I walked out.

(No. No, that is not how it happened at all. It's a vague memory, my visits with the doctor, and troubling; I cried, I think. I was embarrassed. I was afraid to go back. . . .)

After an hour or so, Jed was back at the car, wiping his brow. He asked if I had ever felt sorry for men when I was a boy, like him. (I never did; I always only felt sorry for myself.)

He said he thought Timothy was sick and he did not wish to see him again. Oh, I envied Jed—he really did have sharp, healthy instincts.

*　　*　　*

I don't think I can bear Julius one more second. It isn't his
lack of discrimination for what he says—that, I even ad-
mire. What is, as Jed might say, "creepy" is that he does
not seem to engage with me, he does not notice or care
about my response, my opinions, my self. I am invisible to
him. Before Julius rushes off to change for some party
tonight, he tells me, "Well, I saw a movie last night on
television about these twelve people who crashed in an
airplane in some hideous place in Africa or Australia or
somewhere. Maybe Switzerland, because there was snow.
Completely in the middle of nowhere, darling, no phones,
hotels, *nothing*. So, naturally, they were stranded in these
mountains, freezing, and they were starving. I imagine all
they had were those horrid little Salisbury steaks and fried
chicken dinners the airlines serve. And then they had pea-
nuts of course. So, they were starving, and some of these
people, some old man and a nun and someone else, died.
Well, then the question became: should the survivors eat
the people who had died? The pilot said no. One of the
passengers—a *very* attractive actor, I forget his name, but
he used to be big, and everyone has always known he's gay,
gay, gay—well, his character said yes, they should start
frying up the dead people and eating them. To survive.
Isn't that a scream?"

"Well, Julius, I guess people are capable of anything.
And how did the movie end?"

"Well, my dear, that whore Margo and her crack-
addict brother, Hal or Hank or something, came over to
my apartment and made a mess of everything because
they'd got kicked out of their own place. So I didn't get
to see the end. But it is *quite* the dilemma, isn't it? That's
up your alley, Holly. All these deep, ethical sorts of ques-

tions. So, do tell. If you were on a plane that crashed, and you were stranded, and some people perished but some survived—would you eat the dead passengers?''

Dead passengers. *Dead Passengers.* Wasn't that a title of one of Flanagan's novellas? Flanagan has left the café, Flanagan's gone.

''Well?'' Julius blinks ferociously at me.

''Well, Julius. I don't know if I'd eat them. I'd do something to them, though.'' And Julius howls with mean laughter, puts his fingers to his throat, leans back his head, delighted.

Jed

I don't know what Holly thinks happened to us, what he's saying about it now, but I know he was expecting it. He's the one who says you always lose the thing you really love.

Ever since Las Vegas, Holly was the littlest bit different, some way I can't even describe or anything, just different. Angrier or something . . . no, not angry. Tired? Bitter? No. Some combination of things. When we were on the road, I felt we had this great love, this companionship, etc. We fit together, we understood each other. That changed after Las Vegas. So, I have this theory that maybe when I got so sick, Holly didn't love me as much. Maybe when Holly saw me so weak or whatever, it meant something—like bad luck, like one of his omens—about who he thought I was.

And in L.A., I guess we were living a pleasant, okay enough sort of life. We still did our lessons together, usually at night. We'd light candles. It rained a lot. We were quiet.

I didn't like to have sex with Holly anymore, really, but I liked how much he liked to. See, it always seemed like Holly was never passionate about anything, not anything. Even when there was an earthquake in L.A. one time, kind of a big one, actually, Holly's only reaction was to be irritated because it had woken him up. That's what he's like. I think it must come from having a suicidal mother; I mean, when you're a baby, and your mother hates life so much—that has to do something to you. But, about me—I mean, about me naked, about sex with me— Holly *was* passionate in his own kind of way.

Once I asked Holly about safe sex. I'd seen posters and ads on TV about it and everything, and I got curious. "So listen," I said, "how come you never have been using condoms and stuff with me?"

We were on the back porch, Holly in a beat-up old wooden chair and me standing, leaning against the gate. Holly was trying to sketch a picture of me on the back of an envelope. "I have no artistic talent," he said.

"Hey, really, Holly. How come we never practiced safe sex?"

"There isn't any such thing. Sex is *supposed* to be dangerous. Sex is inherently risky."

"How do you know you haven't given me AIDS or something?"

"I don't have AIDS, Jed."

"But you could, I mean, how do you know for sure?"

He held his drawing out and looked at it, closing one eye. "Oh, Jed. God wouldn't be so cruel as to give me AIDS. Not after everything else he's given me."

Which was so stupid and wrong, you know? I walked to the door.

"You've moved, Jed," Holly said. "You've ruined my sketch."

I went inside, but I looked out the window at Holly, watched him shade a bit of my face on the envelope. He seemed so sad and alone, so small. So I was feeling sorry for him, but angry too. I lifted up the window and Holly turned and faced me.

"I guess maybe you just don't really care about me, Holly."

And he kept looking at me for a few seconds, with the weirdest kind of glassy, scared eyes, like he was a little kid who's caught doing something wrong and knows he's in trouble. And then he bowed his head. We didn't talk anymore.

What happened first was Holly taking me to some weird party. We had been in L.A. almost a year—I had turned fifteen. And Holly knew a lot of people there, he was always hanging around this café place and he knew practically everyone who came in, he sat and talked with all these different people. So I started asking him to introduce me to his friends, I wanted to meet someone, I wanted to get around more or whatever.

"They're idiots."

"But I don't know anyone. I just go fuck with these creepy old guys, that's the only people I ever get to meet."

"You have me, Jed."

I mean, what do you say? Sometimes, toward the end there, it seemed like Holly was daring me to hurt his feelings.

A siren whirred. There are always these crazy sirens in L.A.

So, anyway, finally I talked him in to taking me to this party. It was in Beverly Hills. I was really impressed, actually, even though I was pretending not to be. Really an incredible house, modern furniture and everything and all this food. Especially I remember steak tartare, which was weird. Very faggy men at this place, and the women were all dressed in black, with dyed hair, and they had accents. Everyone was talking about art and stuff. People were sniffing cocaine. Holly didn't do any, but he told me I should if I felt like it. I went into this huge bathroom, done all in black tile and mirrors and a pink rug with this fruity guy, Julius, and this woman with a practically shaved head and big earrings, named Victoria. Victoria said, "Are you old enough for this?" but she handed me a straw and a little mirror with the tiny line of coke laid out.

I saw Holly a few minutes later and he asked if I was feeling the drug. I said I was, I started describing how weird everything looked, like things were throbbing and shifting, and I felt like my heart was pumping and stuff. Holly said, "You're faking."

Anyway, Holly had all these friends he hated. But some of this crowd seemed to like me. I was telling this one guy I had been taking my pictures and what I was mostly shooting. So this guy said I should send him some of my work, he'd publish it in his magazine, and I got all excited and everything. Holly said the guy just wanted to fuck me. So that made me feel bad but, also, so what? If I fucked for money, if I fucked for Holly, what was so bad about fucking to get a photo in a magazine? See what I mean?

So, for a few months, I guess you could say I became like the little darling of this weird crowd, and they were

superficial and everything, they weren't the greatest people in the world, but it kind of made me feel good to be
the center of attention. These people had all this money
and they were always talking about their film projects and
art galleries. I got to meet famous people, like writers and
actors, and the gay men ones were always really nice to me
and asked me questions, but then they were pretty snotty
too. And everyone seemed to know who Holly was.

So, around this time I was starting to think kind of bad
things about Holly. I did understand how amazing a person
Holly was. I knew he was completely unique, that there
was no one else like Holly. But I guess being unique isn't
the only thing in life.

I mean, I loved Holly. No one can ever tell me I didn't
really love him or that he forced me into anything. I mean,
people always are talking about boys getting abused by
older men, and the older men are taken to prison or
whatever for fucking with these boys—and I don't know
about all those situations, but I know with me and Holly
it was different. We were just together.

One day, it was boiling hot and we had all the windows
and the doors open and were wearing underwear and
watching an afternoon talk show on TV all about this kid,
this fourteen-year-old girl, who got kidnapped by some
man who was a friend of the family. And the man and the
little girl had sex and everything. So, I wanted to say,
"Hey, that's like us," but I didn't say it, I thought Holly
might not think it was funny. So, they're asking this girl
about it and she starts to cry and she's all traumatized and
everything right there on national TV. Then, they bring
out this psychiatrist guy who's going on about people in
positions of authority—teachers, priests, therapists, etc.—
how it's bad when they have any kind of sexual thing with

the people they're trying to help, and, of course, it's especially bad when it's with children.

Which got me thinking. Holly did have this weird power or something, because he was older, so I depended on him, etc. But, then, I mean, there's power every-where—husbands and wives, cops, priests and teachers, bosses. People want these black-and-white answers all the time, but sometimes things are more complicated than that. I had a certain power over Holly, too, don't forget. It was a relationship; that's what I think.

So, anyway, by this time I knew Holly was a criminal, even though I didn't know the details. Strange people called him on the phone, all hours. He had this huge amount of money, which he kept hidden behind a panel under the bathroom sink. "Did you steal all of this money?" I tried asking. He said he didn't exactly steal it, but he got it out of people.

Which brought up this weird sort of idea, or realiza-tion. Holly had always made it seem like I had to hustle with these men to support us, we needed the money, and he kept careful accounts of everything I earned. But, as time went on and I saw how much loot he had stashed away, I had this thought that me hustling was something else for Holly, a game, an exciting, daring kind of thing. It wasn't something I had really figured out, it was just vague, and it bothered me. Like, maybe, the thing pushing me forward with the handsome painter that weekend, wanting to be seen but not wanting to. That excitement, that scary, crazy, out-of-control need, was the same thing Holly felt when he set up my appointments, drove me to the men. And especially when he counted out the money I brought home. He was kind of getting off on me.

We didn't really have fights, exactly, not the way Lila

fought with her husbands or the way people do on soap operas. It was more like every time I walked in the house, or in a room where Holly was, I felt this little shiver of disgust for him. He never wanted to do anything. It seemed like he didn't care about anything. I was all crazy, like obsessed, with my photography and I'd say, "Let's go to Venice and shoot some pictures," or "Hey, let's go down to the new mall, or to Santa Monica Boulevard, or drive through Beverly Hills." "Hey," I'd say, "it's almost sunset, come with me while I take my pictures." Holly wasn't interested. He didn't even make excuses. It's like he'd kind of withered away, he'd lost that curiosity he used to have.

Kafka's *Amerika* was the last book we really studied together. I had so many questions. Holly did answer them, and we talked about Prague and he steered me to some other books; but it wasn't like it used to be. He just didn't care anymore. I felt pushed away a little bit. Hurt, I guess. And I kept trying to figure out what had gone wrong. Maybe L.A. wasn't the best place for Holly, because of all his rotten memories. Maybe he was worried about money or something. Then there was his health problem—he called it "the sickness." Nothing was ever diagnosed with Holly, not by a real doctor or anything, and I guess I always assumed it was pretty much in his head. He told me the sickness started when he was a little boy. "And now it has become me."

"Well, is the sickness getting worse, Holly?"

"Of course. It can only possibly get worse."

Also, it seemed like he was taking so many drugs—different pills for all his aches and pains, and half the time he didn't really need them. But they did affect him: he'd be groggy and giggly and lazy, he'd forget things.

And then mostly I wondered, is it me? Am I being hurtful to Holly? Does he resent me or something?

So, I was worried about him, but I was getting annoyed with him, too. Impatient. I mean, he was always coughing, limping, complaining, etc. All of a sudden, he always looked bored; or maybe it wasn't all of a sudden, maybe I was just seeing him in a different light or whatever. I'd come home, Holly would be sitting in his chair, reading his paper. I'd have this view of him from behind, and then I'd find myself hating the back of his head. I remember that so well—just completely hating and despising the back of Holly's head. Which made me feel guilty, of course, but I couldn't help it.

I've always had this strange thing I've wondered, ever since I was the littlest kid. It's: Am I a fake? Or, I mean, Am I really real? I remember being in school, fourth grade, sitting at my desk, and the teacher was doing multiplication tables on the blackboard. I had my math book open in front of me, holding it up a little so the teacher couldn't see that I was hiding another book. I was really reading *Doctor Doolittle's Voyage to the Moon*. Doctor Doolittle was this round little guy who took care of animals in a little English town, and he could communicate with the animals. There was a whole series of a million books about Doctor Doolittle. The books were thick, with hard covers, so you felt like you were reading practically a grown-up book. And Doctor Doolittle had this little boy who worked for him, Tommy Stubbins, and the boy followed him all over the world on these exotic adventures or whatever, talking to animals. They even flew to the moon together. I loved Doctor Doolittle.

So, but anyway, then I looked around at all the other kids. Some were watching the teacher, some were like whispering to each other or whatever, a couple were staring into space or out the window. But they were *there*. They, at least, were in that room. And somehow I couldn't be . . . I was off, like in a dream life of my own.

I'm not explaining this right, I know. I tried to tell Holly about it. He hugged me. It was strange and sudden how he hugged me.

The worst thing, I mean, the thing that was sort of like the beginning of the end was when Holly's friend came to stay with us. Rhoda Because. I thought she was a drag queen or transsexual or whatever, because she had tons of makeup and bright white hair piled on her head and she swayed her hips when she walked. But she actually was a woman, and her voice was so low and husky because she smoked a hundred million cigarettes a day.

Holly sent me to the library one day, told me to take the bus. He said he had a little business to take care of and wanted me to get some books by this writer, Willa Cather. Ever since I started working, we had kept up our studying; but it was different, it wasn't as concentrated or whatever, so actually, I was rather glad Holly had something he wanted me to learn. Anyway, I came back with these Willa Cather novels and when I walked in the house, sitting in that wicker chair which I had painted white and green was this friend of Holly's, wearing a black miniskirt. Holly introduced us. Rhoda Because stood up and kind of wriggled over to me and patted my hair. She had really long red fingernails. She said to me, ''Aren't you so *sweet*?'' Then she turned to Holly, she laughed and put her fingers to her lips and said, ''Holly, now you've gone too far.''

Well, anyway, I don't know, she was nice enough to me. But it seemed like she didn't take me too seriously,

like I was just some little kid to her. I mean, Holly and I
had been companions now for all this time, and suddenly
here's this very loud, tacky kind of person in the middle
of our house. I guess I felt like she was butting in. I guess
I was jealous or whatever.

They'd known each other for years, they had both
been hookers when they were kids. And Rhoda Because—
of course that wasn't her real name—had played in some
artsy underground films or whatever. Then she got married and had a kid who died somehow, I'm not sure of the
whole story. The two of them stayed up late getting drunk
together every night, and then Holly would stumble in to
our bed and pass out in his clothes.

In the morning, we had to tiptoe around because of
Rhoda Because, still asleep on the foldout couch with this
black mask over her eyes. Then, when she got up, like at
noon or whatever, she'd sit around drinking coffee with
bourbon splashed into it, filling the house with smoke,
talking on and on . . . I can't even remember what about.
Men, I think. All these men who had been mean to her.
Relationships—she whined on and on about relationships.
And money. Everyone in the whole world owed Rhoda
Because money.

And, I don't know, it seemed like she was pretty
loaded most of the time; she had a trillion billion pill
bottles all stuck into these little bags with zippers, and then
those bags were in bigger bags. Once a day at least she'd
nod off with a cigarette between her fingers; her fingers,
and her arms too, were covered with scars or scabs or
whatever, little rough, gray spots. I'd look at her skin
sometimes and know I should feel sad, sorry for her. But,
I was only ever mad.

I really hated her, and I'm not sure why, I can't say.

I found myself actually kind of gritting my teeth all the time. I'd come home, she'd be sort of lounging around, her hair all messed up. She'd smile at me—acting like she liked me—but all I saw were these insincere, yellow teeth.

It hit me finally that who I really hated was Holly. It was like he disappeared around her. He made her pots of coffee and laughed at her jokes, spent all this time with her. He even stopped driving me to my appointments—he just gave me cab fare, told me to be careful. So it was kind of like *I* disappeared too. I thought she was pretty snotty to me, actually; she didn't say anything mean, it was more that she kind of ignored me or she'd give me these really condescending kinds of looks. And Holly never would defend me. We'd be having dinner—Rhoda Because was a real pig, shoving food into her mouth really fast and smoking a cigarette at the same time, drinking vodka—and I would try and catch Holly's eye, to connect somehow with him.

So, this creepy Rhoda Because had been with us two weeks. So, one night, a rare night when Rhoda Because was out of the house, Holly and I were alone, folding clothes from the laundry. I said, "You know, I mean, how long is Rhoda Because going to be here, anyway?"

"I'm not sure, Jed."

"Well"—I was pretty mad by this time, it had been building up—"in case you're interested, Holly, I don't like her very much. I don't think she likes me either."

"She's a guest. She's had some trouble."

"Well, whatever. I mean, that's fine and everything. But, in case you're interested, I do live here, you know, and I don't like her at all."

"No. I can see that."

"Well, Holly, I was thinking maybe I should have

some say in things. You know? So, my say in things is that I want Rhoda Because out of here.''

"You should, you should have a say, Jed. I understand.''

"I mean, don't you think she's really sort of despicable?''

After a long minute, after Holly had finished sorting our socks, he said, "Yes. She is sort of despicable.''

So, I took that as an admission, as agreement. I stood up, held out my hands. "Well, okay. Okay, then, Holly. So, why do you want to spend time with a despicable person?''

Holly gave a short laugh. Then he looked directly at me, into my eyes. "Jed. Jed, I don't care who I spend time with.''

Holly and I just looked at each other. I was really upset, I thought the whole situation was so unfair. Unfair to me.

Holly looked sad, weak. And when he looked that way it was so easy for me to just forget my own side of things, to feel . . . I guess it's sympathy. Pity, maybe? Maybe what people think is love is really just pity.

But, I wanted to stay mad; I was right. So I just turned around, like a soldier doing an about-face, and walked away, and before I'd left the room I heard Holly whisper, "I'm sorry.'' But I didn't turn back.

A couple of days later, I came home from the health food store with papayas and juice and stuff. In L.A., because the air's so thick, everything's so smoggy and hot you almost have to eat health food. Anyway, I walked in the house to discover all of Rhoda Because's junk—which had been thrown all over the living room and bathroom for weeks—was completely gone. I asked Holly what happened to Rhoda Because.

"Oh, she left very suddenly, unexpectedly."

As I was putting away our groceries I was thinking, well, good riddance you old bitch. Hope you never come back this way again.

"By ambulance," Holly said. He was reading the L.A. *Times*. "She had a seizure this afternoon."

I just stood there in the kitchen, holding a bag of dried apricots or something. "Well, I mean, is she okay or whatever?"

"Mmm?" Holly looked over at me. "No, Jed. She died."

Turns out Rhoda Because didn't die at all, Holly was just saying that. Just wanted to see my reaction. When I looked so sad and kind of shocked and everything—I mean, I hated that Rhoda Because, but I didn't want her to die—Holly laughed and said: "You really *are* a sincere boy."

I grabbed my Leica and stormed out of the house then, and really slammed that door behind me. I remember running down the steep side of our street and there's a little dead end where everyone in the neighborhood throws their garbage and I just crazily shot pictures of green trash bags and cat shit and beer bottles and everything, all out of focus. See, maybe the year before, maybe even a couple of months before, I would have been all intrigued with Holly's jokes and tests. Or I would have just thought he was mean, or unfair, or crazy, or something; but I still would have thought he was just the most weirdly fascinating person, so smart and deep.

But as time went by . . . I don't know, I felt very guilty

because Holly was just being himself, just being the way he'd always been; but somehow I didn't like him anymore.

We were always honest with each other, we always spoke straight. So, one morning, watching him eat his English muffin, I even told him that being around him was starting to make me feel angry and sick to my stomach. Holly just nodded. "Yes, that's contempt. You're beginning to feel contempt for me. It's inevitable in all relationships—parent-child, lover, sibling. Want half a muffin?"

One night in bed, Holly asked if I wanted to slap him and I laughed. But, he didn't laugh. "You can hit me if you need to, Jed."

I turned on the light. I sat up, put my elbows on my knees, my head in my hands. I heard Holly light a cigarette.

"I want to stop all of this, Holly."

"All of this? What is all of this?"

"Hustling. Fucking for money."

"Well, if you want to stop, stop. You're free."

"What about us?"

"Well, it will cause us some problems, frankly. We'll have to find another source of income I suppose." See, that was his game, that we really did need the money I earned.

"And what about us?" I asked.

"Oh, yes, well, I see what you mean. You want us to stop, too."

"I love you, Holly."

"Thank you."

"But everything's just starting to feel weird to me. Us, I mean."

"You think it's wrong?"

"Not wrong, not wrong."

"Bad?"

"No, not bad. It's like it isn't working anymore. It's

like if I had a shiny new bike, and it was great and everything for a while, but then it broke, it didn't work anymore. And I don't even *want* to fix it."

"That happens so much in life, doesn't it?"

"You're being really mean and everything about this."

"Am I? I'm just listening, I'm just trying to hear what
you're saying."

"I'm saying I want out. We've been together, what,
nearly two years or something?"

"Or something."

"Well, I'm ready to leave now."

"Do you really think so, Jed?"

"Look, Holly, I'm growing up."

"Oh, I see. You're growing up. Well, good-bye
then."

So now I was getting kind of angry, frustrated, irritated, etc. "I mean, Holly, I mean, I just want out of this
crummy little house, driving around to fuck with these
pathetic men. I guess I want out of your life, Holly."

"My sneaky ways and tricky talk. . . ."

"I just feel, I don't know, like trapped in here. This
is no way to live."

"Well, how should one live?"

"I'm not trying to hurt you."

"No. And you *shouldn't* try to hurt me."

"What it boils down to—I'm just ready to stop."

"Well, you're absolutely a free person. So stop."

"I want to do different things, Holly."

"Such as?"

"I don't know."

"Where will you go?"

"I don't know. I've met a lot of people, you know."

"A lot of ridiculous people."

"I'm thinking about San Francisco. I'm thinking I'll head up there or something. I've just maybe kind of outgrown this place."

"Yes. Well, that is reasonable."

"I'm not afraid."

"Well, that's fine then."

"What about you?"

"This is who I am, Jed."

"Well, it's not who I am."

"Isn't it?"

I turned out the light. Holly made slow circles with his cigarette, so the orange end floated through the blackness, and we said nothing. It was rather pretty, it was nice.

That night was chilly. I was wearing pyjama pants and a sweatshirt and Holly asked if I'd take them off. I did. Holly put a hand on each of my shoulders and rubbed, pressed, stroked my whole body, slowly, covering every inch, reaching around and under me, and then he kissed me rather gently on the lips. It was sweet. It felt, I don't know, kind of beautiful but quite sad, too.

"They're going to catch you one day, Holly." The lights were on now and I was loading film into my camera.

He laughed. "They? Who?"

I clicked a picture of him laughing. "I don't know, Holly. The police."

"Whatever for?"

"All this stuff you do, this money you're always getting and—I don't know, all this illegal stuff you're up to."

"I wouldn't worry, Jed. Don't take another picture, no—"

I did though, click click click. I stood up on the bed and got a shot of the top of Holly's head, then fell to my knees. "Okay," I said. "A real portrait. Look serious."

Holly looked right at my lens and I pressed the shutter release. I have that photo of Holly to this day.

I said, quietly, ''You know, this hasn't exactly been a dream life or anything for me.''

''I see. I understand.''

Then, I said, ''Well, if you kidnap anyone else, they'll catch you for that.'' I was sort of making a joke, but then the word *kidnap* sounded cruel, like I was saying our relationship was that kind of thing, and it wasn't, really, so I felt bad.

But Holly had no reaction, he didn't seem hurt, surprised, mad, etc. He only said, ''Oh, they'll never catch me.''

Holly

Rhoda called me one morning, frantic. I was sick of her already. I get sick of everyone sooner or later, particularly that type who get frantic. I never tired of Jed, of course, but was vaguely, uneasily aware that he was reaching the end of his rope with me.

Rhoda had arranged for a ride to her clinic but, predictably, was left standing on the most vulgar and dangerous L.A. corner, attired in impeccably rotten taste, overly madeup, sick from drug withdrawal, quite stood up. Poor Rhoda never had managed to pull herself together. She'd complain, "I couldn't get back up on my feet after the baby died." And I'd say, "Yes, Rhoda, I know, Rhoda."

I did run the errand with her, then dropped her at the house of some other undesirable friend. As it was not yet noon and I knew Jed was out taking his pictures, I impulsively drove to Venice Beach.

With my cane tapping beside me like a third leg, I

walked along the wooden boardwalk, not yet as crowded as I knew it would become later in the day. I'd not been to this place since I was a teenager, hustling. My memories were not good, although the smells of fried food and beer and dead fish were immediately and oddly comforting. Tiny, unkempt houses and shops lined the beach, painted pink or lime green or violet, but the colors were fading. I passed a group of very tan, absurdly muscular men, wearing brief swimsuits, practicing their posing routines. Some kids with bleached hair were roller-skating. A girl had set out a case with handmade earrings for sale and was sitting beside it on a pillow, wearing sandals, strumming a guitar, singing. I saw one young man, whom I pegged as a junkie from his dark clothing, sunglasses, the urgency of his walk; but I was struck by his square, unshaven jaw, his handsome, thin neck.

At Scooter's Quick Lunch Stop I bought a ham sandwich on white bread, wrapped in wax paper, and a bottle of cream soda, tucked these things in my jacket pockets, pulled my hat lower over my eyes.

I leaned against a broken stone railing at the edge of the beach and removed my shoes and socks; with these in hand, I walked unsteadily on my pinkish, tender bare feet across the dirty, tan sand. The sun was still low and hidden behind a pancake of silver clouds. I walked far enough to be away from the distinctness of the beach and boardwalk; it was just a crooked, colorful, meaningless horizon to me now. I felt a delightful small breeze. I faced the soft surf.

I know people think I am bitter. Jed saw bitterness in me, fatalism, some sad resignation. Or perhaps he perceived that was nothing but a posture. I cannot bother to correct any impressions or argue them; I'm too sick.

If I am bitter, though, it is the bitterness of someone who has finally become exhausted with searching.

Two women approached. They did not speak. They watched their feet, which moved with splendid, unplanned togetherness through the sand. I wondered if they might stop and say something to me, something unkind, or if they would laugh at me. The shorter one was carrying a cooler and blankets, the taller held a small beach umbrella and a portable radio from which, as they passed, I could hear a sweet, lonesome violin.

Then I heard drums. I heard deep, hollow notes from giant bamboo reeds. I heard chants of natives, squeals of bats, monkey laughter, and island jungle noises, and saw then an army of naked bodies with shields and spears, their faces painted colors, racing through the waves of the ocean, racing up onto land.

What an imagination! Nothing but a bunch of kids with surf boards. Laughing, headed toward the bar up on the boardwalk.

I folded my hands across my chest, for the wind had risen suddenly, I was chilled. I had not yet actually lost Jed, but I was missing him. I was missing, too, some fast, probably flawed image of Aunt Joy. Missing love. A title for Flanagan, perhaps—*Missing Love*—and it would be his best book.

It must really be the most common human experience, it must be universal, like stubbing a toe, to gaze out at the vastness and mystery of an ocean, as I was doing that morning, and for one clear moment to understand the vastness and mystery of life; and I knew that if they are indeed taking photos from Mars, as Jed once hoped, the last person on earth they'll see is me. And then, too, it is common to forget these fancy philosophies, to feel suddenly hungry or horny or bored, to remember the call one forgot to make, the lover one had fought with and to scurry away from unfathomable powerlessness, from nature, meaning, back to whatever has been a refuge. I walked quickly back to my car, headed home.

> Aschenbach sat near the balustrade, a glass of pomegranate-juice and soda-water sparkling ruby-red before him, with which he now and then moistened his lips. His nerves drank in thirstily the unlovely sounds, the vulgar and sentimental tunes, for passion paralyses good taste and makes its victim accept with rapture what a man in his senses would either laugh at or turn from in disgust.

Sun's nearly gone, so it is dimmer in the café and they have turned on the ceiling lamps, which cast a too-bright glow. I can't last here any longer, anway. Another cup of coffee would be incompatible with my careful dosage of pills, it would counteract the effect. Now, it is getting cold. Flanagan and friends have gone. Julius has gone.

History will show that the most profound of all revolutions was not sparked by the discoveries of Copernicus or Galileo; the real shift in the worldview happened with Freud. Nothing can ever be the same since Psychology. No one can ever really believe in God. No one can ever really fuck anymore. No one can ever escape a mother. Life is self-consciousness.

I used to say all of this to Jed, who would ask, "Well, is that good or bad?"

"Neither good nor bad," I'd reply, and pop my pill.

* * *

So, the event that shaped me, the source of all my meaty trouble, the origin of my sickness, happened in a fast, horrible moment—more horrible for its simplicity, its subtlety.

Is anyone listening?

Mama was due home. She'd been gone a long time. It was summer now, summer again. I sat on the porch. With my green Magic Marker I had drawn a cockeyed face of a cat on my knee.

A tan taxi eased over broken pavement and sprouts of grass, up to the curb. My mouth was open, my eyes were wide.

I saw Aunt Joy's flame of red hair as she got out of the car. She walked around the car, opened the passenger side door to help Mama out. I rose. I dropped my marker and it rolled down the three steps.

Mama was wrapped in a pale yellow blanket. She was wearing brown slippers. Her hair had turned white. I knew it was Mama, but her hair had turned white.

I didn't feel good, suddenly. Warm, tired. My breathing was short.

Aunt Joy led Mama by the shoulders, so slowly up our little walkway, toward me, nearing me. Aunt Joy looked down at Mama's feet as they maneuvered the three steps, as they scraped across the floor to the screen door.

I was waiting. I had been waiting, and now she was home and it had been so long. Mama, though, did not look once at me, not a glance or nod. She glided past—an ill, old thing—someone too fragile or too tragic, too bruised, even to smile at her little boy.

I wasn't feeling good. There was a dull, irregular pulse in my left eye.

From the porch, I looked through the screen and saw

Aunt Joy lead Mama to her room, settle her on the bed inside. I heard Aunt Joy say she'd bring some soup and some crackers and then she told Mama just to rest.

"She's resting," said Aunt Joy to me as I gazed, uncomprehending, through the sooty screen.

"Does my mother know me?" I asked.

"I don't know," Aunt Joy said and turned, pushing fingers wearily through her brilliant hair as she went to the kitchen; and she repeated, "I really don't know."

I've always hated to be alone at night. That typical fear from childhood, that some monster is hiding under the bed, has never really left me.

Jed is not here, and I miss him most at night. I really should have locked Jed in a room, chained him under the porch, tied him to the bedpost. Too late now. I take more pills to sleep.

But the pills—I think it must be the pills—give me some astonishing dreams, furious and vivid. Last night's: a wide, very bright green, flat field. I am walking across it, dragging my cane behind me, forming a line in the dewy grass. Far away, I can see Jed. And I am thinking in my dream, Well, it is a long walk until Jed and I meet in the middle of this field, so I have time to think what I will say to him and what I will do for him. We're walking directly toward each other, but we do not hasten, there is no hurry. I am smiling, in my own way. I have missed Jed.

We have this enormous field, not a tree or house anywhere in sight. No wires, no birds. Just green and me and Jed. It is a sunny, sweet-smelling day. We're closer. How I love Jed. We're closer.

I can never say I'm sorry because I don't know what that means. I can't make a promise, I don't know how to make a promise. We're closer. I'm thinking in this dream, suddenly, how tragic it is that I don't have a thing to give to Jed. We'll meet any moment now, and I have nothing for him. The progress is slow, but we are getting closer.

But, Jed can give to me. Jed can smile, touch me, look at me, ask me a question. When we meet, Jed, will you ask me a question? And then, in a dream, here we are, almost together. Here is Jed, almost before me. Now.

But, it is not Jed. It is someone else. Who does not even look like Jed. Who walks past me, for he does not know me, I am no one to him. I keep walking, I won't look around or follow or wonder. I'm lost.

There must not be a Jed.